# The Mystery of Pheasant Cottage

Patricia St John

Revised by Mary Mills

Illustrated by Gary Rees

Scripture Union

©Patricia M. St John 1977

First published by Scripture Union 1978

This revised edition first published 2001, reprinted 2002

Scripture Union, 207–209 Queensway, Bletchley, Milton
Keynes MK2 2EB

Email: info@scriptureunion.org.uk

Website: www.scriptureunion.org.uk

ISBN 1 85999 512 8

Printed and bound in Great Britain by
Creative Print and Design (Wales) Ebbw Vale.

Scripture Union is an international Christian charity working
with churches in more than 130 countries, providing
resources to bring the good news about Jesus Christ to children, young people and families and to encourage them to
develop spiritually through the Bible and prayer.

As well as our network of volunteers, staff and associates
who run holidays, church based events and school Christian
groups, we produce a wide range of publications and support
those who use our resources through training programmes.

# Contents

# Revised edition

It is over 20 years since the first edition of Patricia St John's *The Mystery of Pheasant Cottage* was published. It has been reprinted many times and has become a classic of its time.

In this new edition, Mary Mills has sensitively adapted the language of the book for a new generation of children, while preserving Patricia St John's skill as a storyteller.

## Chapter One

## Awkward questions

I can clearly remember the first time I really began to wonder about the mystery that surrounded my early life. I was at Infant school, sitting with my friends under the apple tree in the playground. It was a perfect morning in May and we were drinking mugs of milk at breaktime.

"Lucy, why do you live with your gran? Why don't you live with your mum and dad, like everybody else?"

Harvey Chatterley-Foulkes fixed his goggle-eyes on me as he asked his question.

I had to think of an answer quickly, and looked round hopefully for Miss Hunt, my teacher, thinking she would help me, but she had gone to look for someone in the cloakroom. I stared at Harvey, thinking he looked like a fat frog, and said,

"Because I don't. Wipe your mouth, Harvey. You've got a milk moustache." I thought this would make me sound grown-up and confident, but Harvey took no notice.

"But why not?" he insisted, "I mean, where are they? You must have been born from someone."

There was silence. If I said, "I don't know," they would all laugh at me, and I might cry. Now, all eyes were fixed on me, waiting for my answer.

"Perhaps they're dead," said Mary, cheerfully.

"Or perhaps they've run away and left you," breathed Janie.

"Or perhaps they're divorced," broke in Billy, who seemed to know all about it.

I looked round desperately and breathed a great sigh of relief, for Miss Hunt was coming across the playground. I went over to her and felt safe, but Harvey was still determined to find out about my private affairs.

"Miss Hunt," he squeaked excitedly, "*Why* does Lucy live with her gran? I mean, why hasn't she got a dad and..."

Miss Hunt's clear voice soon silenced him.

"If I had a gran like Mrs Ferguson I shouldn't mind too much if I had parents or not; she's as good as a mum and dad rolled into one. You're a lucky girl, Lucy. My gran died when I was a baby. Now, wipe your mouth, Harvey, you've got a milk moustache. And now, everybody listen... as it's the first of May..."

Everyone immediately forgot about me being parentless as we fixed our eyes on Miss Hunt, wondering what delight she was going to surprise us with because it was the first of May.

"Because it's the first of May," she repeated, "instead of going back in the classroom for maths, we're all going for a walk up to the spinney on the hill to pick kingcups – they're just out."

There was a shout of joy as sixteen joyful children raced towards the meadow. Miss Hunt walked behind, and I trotted quietly beside her, still feeling rather shaken.

I knew now that Harvey's question had been there for a long time, buried deep and never asked. Now, all of a sudden, everyone had asked it, and there was no answer.

I knew that I had not always lived at Pheasant Cottage with Gran. A long time before that there had been somewhere else, where a very tall man had carried me in his arms, and I remember very clearly that he had once gone down on all fours and let me ride on his back. As I grew older, I used to wonder if he could have been my father, but, strange to say, I had never asked.

"I'll ask Gran today," I said to myself, and then forgot all about it in the delight of the outing. Miss Hunt was in front now, because the hill was steep for small legs. She looked like the Pied Piper with all her class puffing and hurrying behind her, while she called back exciting instructions.

"See how many different kinds of wild flowers you can find... not all dandelions, Sally! Look very quietly in the hedges – you might see a nest... Harvey, stop chattering! We want to listen to the birds, and you are frightening them all away. Now, stand still, everybody... you, too, Lizzie, stop jumping up and down! Now, very quiet... Can anyone hear that thrush singing?"

Then we plunged into the oak wood, and I was the first to spot a gleam of gold in the shadows and shout, "Kingcups!"

Everyone broke into a charge through the undergrowth, but Miss Hunt shooed us back onto the path so that we didn't get stuck in the swamp. But there were plenty of flowers to be reached from the path and we returned home later with muddy feet and pollen-powdered noses.

Parents were waiting by the schoolroom door, and one by one the children went home, clasping their golden bunches. I lived a long way out and it was four o'clock before Miss Hunt put me on the school bus.

Gran was standing at the bus stop with Shadow, our black Labrador, straining at his lead and barking for joy because he knew I was coming. We usually chased each other madly home, but Shadow must have been disappointed that afternoon because I did not feel like playing. I walked quietly beside Gran, hugging my kingcups; and then, suddenly, I asked my question.

"Gran, why do I live with you and Grandpa? Didn't I ever have a mum and dad? Most of the other children have them."

It seemed very quiet after I had spoken. I could hear a bee buzzing in the lilac tree and a blackbird singing. At last Gran answered.

"Your mummy was our dear daughter Alice, Lucy. She died when you were a tiny baby, and there was no one else to look after you, so Grandpa and I took you as our own little girl."

"But didn't I have a daddy?" I persisted. "And why didn't he look after me? Is he dead too?"

There was a long silence while I waited confidently for the answer, because I knew Gran always spoke the truth.

"He went right away," said Gran slowly, "and we never saw him again. He would not have looked after you properly, Lucy. You belong to us now, and always will, just as though you were our own little girl. Look, there's Grandpa! He's seen us."

We had reached our garden, and by the way she changed the subject and pressed her lips together, I knew that I was not expected to ask any more questions ever again. I did not mind. A delicious smell of baking came from the cottage, and Grandpa waved from his vegetable patch, his rosy face beaming a welcome. Home was a perfect place. What did I want with a father? I really didn't need one!

Yet somehow that old far-away memory puzzled me and wouldn't go away. For if that tall man *had* been my father, then he could not have been completely bad, or he would not have held me in his arms, nor would he have gone down on all fours and let me ride on his back. But it was a puzzle without an answer, and for five whole years I never mentioned it again to anyone.

## Chapter Two

## Guide camp

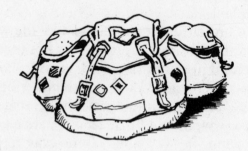

Those five years passed very quickly, and life was happy and exciting. I loved living in the countryside, watching the changing of the seasons. I never much minded being an only child, or not doing the things that the other children did.

Sometimes, when the girls at school laughed at me because I'd never seen the sea, I would grow restless and wondered whether I would ever travel or do anything different from going to school, coming home and going to church on Sundays. I did not see how I could, really, because my grandparents were growing older every year, and Grandpa, who had been head gardener at the castle on the nearby Eastwood Estate for thirty years, only had a small pension. They were perfectly content to remain in their cottage, and, apart from occasionally visiting relatives in Birmingham, they had no wish to take holidays, and could not, in any case, because of having to look after the chickens. And, except when my friends made fun of me, I was content, too, content to play in the woods and climb the hills, to read, and to scribble stories about children who went on long journeys and travelled to all the countries I learned about in geography lessons. I had my own jobs to do in the cottage and garden, too, and the days never seemed long enough.

Sometimes my best friend Mary came to spend the day and I would take her on to the Estate. But Mary was a sturdy, practical child who preferred to arrive somewhere than just to wander. She would often say, "Where are we going, Lucy?" which really annoyed me. My unchanging reply probably annoyed her, too. "We're not going anywhere; we're just walking!" And after a time we would turn back, and play games in the garden. I really liked Mary, but she belonged to my school world, and my woods and countryside bored her.

But from all my happy childhood memories, one event stands out, clear and unforgettable, and that is the Whitsun Guide Camp in the Cotswolds when I was eleven years old. When Gran told Captain I could go, I was so excited that I hardly slept for two nights. And when we actually set off in the bus with our rucksacks and bedding, I could hardly speak. I sat squeezing my clasped hands between my knees, bottling up my joy, because living with elderly people had made me rather a quiet child. But gradually, as we travelled for hours through leafy lanes, I relaxed. We sang, we chattered, we giggled, we ate sandwiches and drank lemonade out of bottles; and then we were there, high on a hill at the edge of a great beech wood, overlooking the Gloucester plain, and Captain and Lieutenant were showing us where to put up our tents, and how to light a fire.

That holiday was everything I had hoped it would be. I shared a tent with Mary, and every waking hour was thrilling, from the moment we crawled out into the sweet-smelling morning to the moment we snuggled into our sleeping bags in the dark, shrieking in pretend terror when the owls hooted in the woods behind us. But I remember most vividly the early morning when I woke before anyone else and, slipping on my jumper and shoes, crept out into the waking world. The sun had not long risen; a cuckoo called from the beeches. Captain was up and wandering about, and she saw me.

"Lucy," she said, "would you like to dress and take a message to the farm for me? Straight through the wood and climb over the stile and cross the hayfield. You'll find them milking the cows. Ask them to save us fifteen fresh eggs and we'll fetch them later."

I was slipping on my dress when Mary's tousled head appeared out of her sleeping bag. She blinked at me.

"Where are you going?" she yawned. "Shall I come too?"

"No, no," I replied hurriedly, "I shan't be long. I've got to go to the farm with a message. I've got to go now, at once. You can come and meet me if you like." I shot outside, for this was my special expedition and I had to go alone. I ran through the sunlit wood, climbed over the stile and saw the hayfield – a tangled mass of wild flowers, all sparkling with dew.

I went mad! I flung my shoes backwards over the stile and leaped and danced barefoot along the path, the flowers tickling my legs. I laughed, and clapped my hands, carried away with the joy of being alive on such a morning, loving the feel of the cold grass between my toes. Then, having delivered my message, I turned back and walked more slowly, wanting this hour to last and last. But it was not to be. Mary was trotting towards me, and by the look on her round face, I knew she had a secret to tell me.

"Lucy," she began mysteriously, "do you know what?"

"What?" I answered.

"Well, I came to meet you through the wood, and Captain and Lieutenant were standing by the stile."

"So what?"

"Well, they *saw* you!"

"I don't care."

"Yes, but Lucy, they talked about you; I heard them. They didn't see me, 'cos I waited behind a tree and I *heard* them, Lucy."

I was silent, desperately curious to know, but I wasn't going to show it!

"Lucy, shall I tell you what they said about you?"

"What, then?"

"Captain said," – and here Mary's voice changed to sound like a grown-up's – "'Fancy good little

Lucy going all wild like that! There's more in that child than meets the eye.' And Lieutenant said, 'Oh, Lucy's got plenty in her. Her teacher says her essays are brilliant. She needs to get away from those grandparents of hers occasionally, and start living.' That's what they said, Lucy. There was more but I can't remember it all, and anyhow they turned round and saw me."

"How silly," I replied, rather crossly, "I live just as much as they do." But somehow the sparkle had gone out of the day, and all that morning while we ate breakfast and tidied, and swam in the river, I puzzled over their remarks. What was wrong with being good? And what was wrong with my grandparents? And what had I been doing all these eleven years except living? I supposed that they said it because I hadn't done all the things the others had done, and because I'd never been to the sea. But after all, they knew nothing about my real life, and they'd never even set foot in the Eastwood Estate. I felt rather cross all day, and they must have wondered what was the matter with me, until the delight of cooking sausages on the campfire drove the whole thing out of my mind.

But it had stirred up all the old questions. I was different.

That night I lay awake for a long time, with Mary snoring beside me, and listened to the owls, and the rustle of the beech leaves, and tried to remember the face of the tall man who had gone down on all fours. But it was no good. It had gone for ever.

## Chapter Three

# A letter arrives

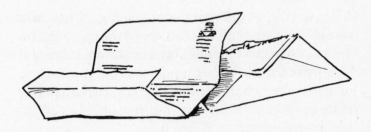

Whitsun camp was over, but time sped on so fast that I seldom looked backwards or forwards, but just enjoyed each new day. Once again summer blazed into autumn and this year I moved up into secondary school.

Once again the snow fell as a white blanket over the hills. Again I collected fir cones, and roasted chestnuts, and made secret Christmas presents. Again I heard the bleat of the first lamb at twilight, and smelt the warm south wind stirring the buds, and knew that spring was on the way. The countryside was a picture of green and gold and blossom.

And then it was the last day of the Easter term. Proper lessons were over and everyone was fidgety and longing for the holidays. Miss Bird, our

English teacher, was reading us a poem, but the window was wide open, we could hear the doves cooing, and the sheep calling their lambs, and no one was really paying attention.

Miss Bird closed the book, stepped to the blackboard and wrote "SUMMER HOLIDAY" in large letters. There was a stir of interest; a few heads looked up.

"You will be planning your summer holidays soon," she announced, "so this is a competition for you to try this holiday, and next term there will be a prize for the best entry. You can write a story, or tell about what you did last year, or what you plan to do this year. Anything you like, but try to get the feel of summer into it."

She looked round at our blank faces. "The feeling of summer seems to be rather a sleepy one," she said with a smile. "Let's collect some ideas and write them on the board. Mary, when I say 'summer holiday', what do you think of?"

Mary jerked to attention. "Er..." she began, "Er... hot... and... ice cream..."

"Yes, all right. Somebody else? Jennifer?"

"Swimming... the beach... donkeys..."

"Punch and Judy show... bingo..."

"Tennis."

"Camping in our caravan."

"Riding my pony..."

Miss Bird was writing rapidly. She turned and faced the thoroughly awakened class.

"Yes, that's right, but what about the places you go to? Anna, where did you go for your last summer holiday?"

"We toured Scotland in our car."

"And what was Scotland like in the summer?"

"Oh, mountains and lakes, and it rained and the car broke down. We saw some castles, and battlefields and things and we watched for the Loch Ness Monster all one day, but no luck!"

Miss Bird gave a small sigh and looked at me.

"Lucy?" she asked.

Somebody gave a little titter, and Mary sprang to my rescue. "Lucy never goes away," she explained. "Her grandparents can't take holidays because..."

"That will do," interrupted Miss Bird. "Summer is here at home too, not just in the holiday places. Besides, Lucy did go on holiday. She went to the Whitsun Camp. Can you tell us about summer in the Cotswolds, Lucy?"

I closed my lips tightly and scowled at my teacher. Why should she ask me? She knew I never went anywhere. Then I glanced at her face and realized she was not making fun of me at all. She really wanted my help. She and I felt the same about summer. I stared out of the window and tried to remember. Summer in the Cotswolds!

"The smell of honeysuckle and new mown hay," I began slowly, "and that sort of shiny light coming through the beech leaves at sunset so all the leaves look separate... seeing stars through a hole in the tent... and the dew on the flowers in the early morning all sparkly... and swimming in the river... kingfishers came out of a hole in the bank and we swung on the willow branches..."

Memories were flooding up, and I could have gone on for ever. Then I suddenly noticed the astonished faces of the other girls gaping at me, and I went red and stopped. Miss Bird had her back to us, and I had never seen her write so fast before. The silence was broken by the bell announcing it was time for break.

"You really did save the situation," said Mary admiringly as we drank our milk. "I just couldn't think of anything but ice creams. I can't think how you manage to be so poetical, Lucy! I should think you'd get the prize easily." I doubted it, for how could my Cotswold experiences compare with touring Scotland by car, or even going to the sea? I felt restless as I wandered home from the bus stop that afternoon. I had recently been reading a poem called *The Forsaken Merman,* all about the sea. I wished I could see the sea! What did "wild white horses" look like, and where did the great tides come from? I felt a strange stirring at the heart of me, a reaching out for change.

I was thinking so hard as I walked up the path that I failed to call out my usual greeting. I stepped quietly into the passage and was about to go into the room where my grandparents were sitting with their backs to me, and I could not help hearing what they said. And having heard, my heart seemed to miss a beat, and I stood as though turned to stone.

"But Elsie," said my grandfather gently, "she will *have* to know soon. She is twelve years old, and after all, he is her father."

"But not yet, not yet," cried my grandmother. "There are still almost two years to go. Anything may happen in two years."

I stepped back very softly and crept out through the front door. They must not know that I had heard. I wanted to run away and hide in the wood, and think and think, but Shadow saw me from the kitchen, and came charging to meet me, slobbering on my feet, wagging his tail and jumping up to greet me. There was nothing for it but to step back inside, just in time to see Gran fold a letter and slip it into the top drawer of her writing desk. But they greeted me as usual and I helped to get tea ready and we sat down to my favourite meal of faggots. The sun streamed in through the window and it should have been a happy, chatty tea as we caught up on the news of the day, but somehow we were all strangely silent. It seemed as though some shadow had come between us and I was almost glad when the meal was over.

"Any homework tonight?" asked Gran.

"No, Gran," I answered. "Tomorrow's the last day of term so we don't do proper lessons. Can I go out for a bit when we've washed up?"

She looked at me with a strangely tender expression.

"Grandpa and I will see to the washing-up tonight, love," she answered. "You run along now, with Shadow. It's a beautiful evening; but come back before sunset."

Grandpa walked to the gate with me and asked where I was going, but I just pointed vaguely up the hill. I wanted to get away by myself, and I sped up the steep slope to the left of the house and flung myself into an old grassy trench where the Ancient Britons were meant to have made a last stand against the Romans. Shadow came and rested his nose against my arm. In front of me, over the rim of the trench lay the great plain. Every road was lit up by the light of the sunset and seemed to run purposefully to the horizon. Every river was a shining ribbon. It looked like a bright clear map, and I suddenly realized what a vast place the world was! So many roads leading away from the safe shelter of my little home – such far, far distances!

What was I to do? If I asked, they would probably not tell me, and anyhow they didn't want me to ask. But I had to know, because he was my father, and I was his daughter, Lucy. Besides, I was twelve years old – old enough to be trusted. Even Grandpa recognised that, but Gran always had the last word, so that didn't help. Then as I lay there, chewing a bracken shoot and watching the sun sink towards the far Welsh mountains, an idea came to me – an idea so wicked that I gasped, and felt my face flush crimson.

I would stay awake until my grandparents were asleep, and then I would creep down, find the letter in the drawer, and read it. I would see the address, and find out where my father was, and what it was all about. Of course I knew perfectly well what Gran thought about people who eavesdropped, and looked at letters that didn't belong to them, but I decided it just couldn't be helped. "After all," I argued with myself, "this letter, in a sense, it *does* belong to me, because it's my father." Then I realised that the sun was sinking below the rim of the world and I jumped up, and raced down across the slippery grass, scattering the sheep in all directions. Grandpa was at the gate, peering short-sightedly down the road.

Evenings at the cottage were cosy times. We sat round the fire in winter, but on warm spring evenings we sat by the open window, and Gran read aloud – mostly from the shabby old books she had loved as a child, such as *Heidi* or *The Secret Garden*. At this time we were half-way through *David Copperfield*, and Dora and Steerforth and the Peggoty family had become part of my life. I could hardly wait from evening to evening to hear the next chapter.

But tonight I did not want to sit quietly with my grandparents in the soft circle of light, as though there was nothing the matter, and even little Em'ly's troubles seemed small and unimportant in comparison with my own. I felt outside the circle, a deceiver, and the loneliness of it was almost more than I could bear. To their great surprise and disappointment, I pretended to be sleepy and crept miserably up to my bedroom.

## Chapter Four

## A shocking discovery

How was I going to keep awake? This was my big problem. If I could have stayed dressed it would have been easier, but I had to get into bed, because Gran always came in to say goodnight to me. I had been taught to say my prayers before I went to sleep, and I usually rushed through them without really thinking what they meant. But tonight I found it really difficult – how could I ask God to forgive me for the things I had done wrong when I was just about to do something very, *very* wrong? In the end, I gave up.

When Gran came in, she put her hand on my forehead and asked if I felt all right.

"Yes, thank you," I answered.

"Are you sure, Lucy?" She lingered, as though she didn't want to leave me. "Have you got a headache? How about a drink of hot chocolate?"

This was supposed to be a big treat, but my stomach seemed tied in knots, so I just smiled, and shook my head and closed my eyes. She went away slowly and I knew she was watching me from the door. But at last I heard her footsteps going downstairs, and then I sat up and looked around.

Perhaps an exciting adventure story would help keep me awake. I dared not switch on the light but I had a torch, and by its light I tiptoed to my bookcase. I turned the pages of one book after another, but nothing seemed exciting except the letter in the desk, and all adventure seemed boring compared with the adventure of creeping downstairs and solving the mystery of my own life. As I sat down by the open window and leaned my arms on the sill, my heart ached. Our safe little home, and Gran and Grandpa and me had seemed so secure and happy till now. Why did this mysterious shadow have to come between us and spoil everything? I nearly decided to forget about that letter, to cuddle down and just go to sleep... but no! I *must* find out, and this was probably my last chance. I leaned against the wall and dozed for a while, and then woke with a start, for my grandparents were coming upstairs.

I dived into bed, and, as I had thought she would, Gran came in and stood over me, with a torch in her hand.

"She's gone off all right," I heard her whisper, "but mark my words, Herbert, there's something the matter with the child."

I could hear Grandpa's distressed murmur, and the click of their door shutting. I staggered up and down in my room for ages, waiting for the line of light under their door to disappear. In another ten minutes or so I listened at the keyhole, and could hear Gran's steady snoring and knew that my time had come.

I tiptoed downstairs and boldly switched on the light in the sitting room. I was shivering with guilty excitement as I pulled open the drawer. The letter I wanted was not lying on the top; Gran must have hidden it, and I had no idea what it looked like, so I thumbed through the pile glancing at the addresses. They were mostly bills or letters from Gran's sister in Birmingham, or Grandpa's nephew in Stockton-on-Tees, nothing mysterious until I had nearly reached the bottom of the bundle – and there was an unusual sort or letter with the address printed at the top:

"Her Majesty's Prison,
Greening."

I stood frozen, rooted to the spot, staring at the address, and only after a long time did my eyes move down to the actual letter.

"Dear Mr and Mrs Ferguson," it began, "As the time of my imprisonment will soon be over, I am writing to you about the guardianship of my daughter, Lucy. I am very grateful…"

I was concentrating so hard on what I was reading that I had stopped noticing anything, even the footsteps on the stairs and the opening of the door. It was only when he was right in front of me that I realised Grandpa was standing there, and I had been caught in the act. I thrust the letter behind my back and burst into frightened, defiant tears.

"Lucy, Lucy, my dear child, whatever is the

matter?" whispered Grandpa, shutting the door very carefully.

I gulped and looked at him pleadingly, and I suddenly realized that there was nothing to be afraid of. This was no policeman catching a criminal red-handed, but a distressed little old man in a very shabby dressing-gown, who couldn't even see what I was doing because he'd left his glasses upstairs.

"You're shivering, child," he said. "I'm going up to your room to get a blanket. Put on the kettle, Lucy, and let's have a cup of tea."

A cup of tea was Grandpa's cure for everything. He came tiptoeing down a few moments later and wrapped me up warm. I stopped shivering and sobbing, and relaxed. I could see that he was very anxious not to wake Gran, and not until we were both sipping steaming cups of tea did he remember to ask me what I was doing.

He had not noticed the letter at all. He had just seen the light shining from the window and crept downstairs to turn it out. But my secret was too heavy and shocking to carry alone any longer. I needed Grandpa's help, so I leaned against him and told him all about it.

"You see, Grandpa, I know it's wrong to read other people's letters, but I had to know. He's my father, and I'd always wondered, only Gran would never tell me."

"No, it wasn't right," said Grandpa, "and I'm glad I came; but maybe we should have told you sooner, or maybe you should have asked us again instead of trying to find out alone. But in any case, it's high time you knew, although there is nothing to be afraid of. There is still quite a long time to go, if he does the whole sentence, and by that time you'll be nearly fourteen, and you'll be allowed to choose for yourself. I don't reckon any court of law would force you to go with your father against your will. We can't stop him seeing you, and he can visit you here."

"But does he want me?" I asked. "I've only seen the beginning of the letter."

"Well now, yes, he seems to want you," replied Grandpa gently, taking the letter out of my hand. "But we've consulted solicitors, Lucy, and he couldn't take you from here, unless you wanted to go, which of course you wouldn't. He wouldn't be a good father for you... in fact I'm afraid he's a very bad man."

"What did he do?" I asked. "Was I there?"

"Yes," said Grandpa, and he spoke very sadly. "It all happened after you were born and after our dear, dear Alice died. She met him at a friend's house, and he soon wanted to marry her. But your grandmother didn't feel it was right, and she wouldn't agree to them getting engaged. He was an unsettled kind of chap, so they just ran away together and got married on their own. They went to Spain. He had a guest-house there, or some such thing, and we never saw our daughter again. She died when you were born."

Grandpa's voice trailed off sorrowfully and he seemed to have forgotten about me. I gave his arm a small shake.

"I'm sorry, Grandpa," I whispered, "but what happened next? I mean, what happened to me?"

"We begged him to send you home to us, but he never answered our letter. I believe he loved your mother very much and was heartbroken when she died. The second time we wrote, it was sent back to us. He had left that address and no one knew where he had gone."

"But where was I, Grandpa? Did he take me with him?"

"Oh yes, but we don't know much about the next three years. I believe he drank too much, and got mixed up with some drug business, helping to bring drugs up through Spain into France. Then he came back to England and the police were waiting for him. It was all in the papers, but to tell you the truth, Lucy, I don't really understand it. It was about that time that he brought you to us."

"Oh! So you've seen him?"

"Oh yes; he arrived in a taxi, all unexpected, with you in his arms, and asked us to look after you for a while. I think he knew he was about to be sent to prison, but he didn't tell us so at the time. We had never seen him much before, but there was no mistaking you – such a funny little thing you were, and the image of your dear mother – the same thick, curly hair, the same grey eyes..."

"But my father, Grandpa! Did he love me?"

"Oh yes – there was no doubt about that. You'd been well cared for, too, and you talked a mixture of English and Spanish. He said you'd had a Spanish nanny... he wouldn't stay or tell us much. He just put you into Gran's arms. You clung to him and cried at first, but then you fell asleep. When you woke up next morning you might have belonged to us all your life. You were just three and a half."

"But tell me about my father, Grandpa. Didn't he ever come back?"

"No; a few days later it was all in the papers, and he wrote telling us he'd got a ten year sentence, and asking us to care for you. Your Gran wasn't surprised – said she'd known he was a bad lot from the beginning, and we must make sure you were never told. But when he comes out you'll have to know, Lucy, and maybe it's best you know now. But I sometimes wish, for Alice's sake, we'd done differently…"

"What was she like, Grandpa?"

"She took after your Gran, Lucy. Gran was the village school mistress when I married her, and there were many people who said I wasn't good enough for her. They were right, for I was never very good at school work, but she seemed satisfied. We weren't very young and we only had Alice, and she was the spitting image of your Gran… only more so, in a way. Your Gran always loved reading, but Alice had a real passion for books and learning. She'd dance round the garden saying poetry to herself and lie there under the rowan tree in summer, scribbling away. We managed to send her to college, too. She got degrees and all the rest of it, but she hated being away from the cottage for long, and the hills. She was always coming back… until she met him. You're very like her, Lucy, and we don't want…"

"Herbert, what in heaven's name are you doing down there?" Gran suddenly called in a loud whisper from the top of the stairs and we both jumped guiltily to our feet, and thrust our tea cups in a corner.

"I'm coming, Elsie," replied Grandpa, but I seized his arm.

"Are you going to tell her?" I faltered.

"Oh yes, of course," murmured Grandpa, hurrying to the door, and I realized that he'd never kept a secret from her in his life and would not start now. I kept tight hold of his arm as we climbed the stairs.

"And *may I* ask what Lucy is doing?" Gran said crossly, looking rather fierce and unfamiliar in her hair curlers. "Is there a reason...?"

"Yes, dear, there is... I'll tell you all about it. Lucy, go back to bed." And to my great astonishment, I saw Grandpa guide a speechless Gran into the bedroom, and the door was slammed on me.

I climbed into bed, shivering, but it was a long, long time before I went to sleep. Wonder, shock, excitement, regret, and a strange cold fear of the future kept me awake, for one day this bad man was going to reappear and I was going to have to know what to do. I tossed and turned, till a cock crew far away and some sheep bleated up on the hill. A bird trilled the first few notes of the dawn chorus, and, though the stars were still out, another spring morning had begun. I was suddenly drowsy, and my confused thoughts quietened. I just saw a man, heartbroken because his wife had died, kissing a baby daughter goodbye. I imagined him sitting in a dark, lonely dungeon, for ten years, and I'd never known. Perhaps I could have comforted him, even if he was such a bad man. I buried my face in my arms and wept, and the next thing I knew was the sun streaming into my bedroom, and Gran standing by my bed with a cup of tea.

"Wake up, Lucy," she said. "I let you sleep on. But you'll have to hurry to catch the bus."

But there was no afternoon school, and, as soon as we'd washed up the dinner things, Gran and I settled down in the garden, and I heard exactly what Gran thought about children who sneaked downstairs at night to read other people's letters, and said they were sleepy when they were not. By the time she had finished I felt too ashamed of myself to ask her any of the questions I wanted to ask.

"Sorry, Gran," I said, because that is what she expected me to say. And then I quite surprised myself by adding, "But I had to know sometime, didn't I? After all, he is my father, and I am twelve years old."

She stared at me, but the sharp answer I expected never came. "Lucy," she said, and to my amazement her voice trembled, "I hope you will never have to have anything to do with him. No one could take you away from us now... not after all these years."

I stared back at her and saw that her eyes were full of fear – fear because she loved me, and because the shadow of losing me had hung over her, day and night, for eight years. I flung my arms round her neck and hugged her. Then I ran off into the wood with Shadow at my heels.

It was quiet in the wood and now that the first shock of discovery was over, I wanted to think. Strange new thoughts were surging up inside me. I ran through the wood anemones and primroses to the edge of the trees where a golden stream ambled along. All over the bank wild daffodils pierced the dead oak leaves and catkins danced above my head, scattering pollen on my hair. Here I sat, resting my chin on my knees, and realized I'd changed. Over the last twenty-four hours I'd begun to grow up in a hurry.

Gran was a very fair woman. She always listened to what I had to say, and when she told me off I usually knew in my heart that what she said was right. But today I was not so sure. I felt less ashamed of my "creeping and peeping", as she called it, than I had expected to, because it seemed to me that the letter hadn't really belonged to Gran at all. My father was mine, and the news belonged to me, and it was up to me alone to decide what I was going to do about it.

## Chapter Five

# Making friends with Don

It was warm and peaceful where I sat in the wood.
I could just hear the brook gurgling slowly and the
birds cooing excitedly as they nested in the trees
behind me. Then suddenly Shadow lifted his head
and growled. I turned to see a boy limping along
the bank – a pleasant-looking boy about my own
age, with thick brown hair.

"Hi!" he called out. "Do you happen to have a
tissue or something?"

I fished up the sleeve of my sweater and brought
out a rather grubby hanky. He sat down beside me
and held out his foot. It was badly cut and bleeding freely.

"Go down to the stream and hold it in cold water
first," I said, remembering my Guide's first-aid
course, and he obeyed, sitting on a stump and

dangling his foot in the water. Then I tied it tightly with my handkerchief and we sat watching to see if the blood would seep through or not. I had had little to do with boys since I left primary school, and I was usually shy of them, but a boy in trouble was different.

"How did you do it?" I asked.

"I trod on some broken glass in the stream back there. I was paddling."

"But you're not supposed to be in the stream at all. This is a pheasant reserve and it's a private estate."

"Then what are *you* doing here?" he asked, smiling at me.

"Oh, I belong here," I replied grandly. "My grandfather was head gardener at the Castle for thirty years."

"Really?" replied the boy. "But isn't it rather boring playing in this great place all alone? I mean, wouldn't it be more fun if there was someone else?"

I'd never really thought about it.

"Well, yes," I replied slowly, "I suppose it would. Do you often come here?"

"This is my first time. We've only just come to live here. I didn't come in through the gate. I came from the valley and I got under the barbed wire at the back. I belong to a natural history club at school and I'm doing a project on wildlife in this county. These woods are the perfect place to watch and I'm very careful about pheasants. I want to dam the stream lower down, to make a pool, then more animals would come to drink – specially early in the morning. Oh, gosh! Look at my foot!"

The handkerchief was saturated with blood. Something had to be done at once.

"Where do you live?" I asked.

"Down in Eastbury. But I couldn't walk as far as that. I might bleed to death!"

"Well, come up to my house, and my Gran will bandage it and phone for a taxi. We live by the main gate. It's only about ten minutes' walk."

"Won't she mind? I'm a trespasser, remember."

"Oh, no! She's not interested in pheasants. Grandpa is, but he's out in the greenhouse, and he's so interested in his tomatoes that he won't think to ask what you're doing. Come on!"

It took us nearly twenty minutes to reach the house, because the injured foot was very painful. Fortunately he had a knife, and we cut a stout stick for him to lean on. He limped bravely along and as we walked, we talked, and I learned quite a lot about him.

His name was Donald, but he said I could call him Don, and he was twelve years old. His father had taken over the Royal Midland Hotel just before Christmas, and was doing well with it. Don was obviously tremendously proud of his father. He hadn't any brothers and sisters, and went to boarding-school, so he hadn't made any friends in the town yet. We had nearly reached home when he turned to me and said, "And what about you? What were you doing all by yourself?"

"Oh, just thinking."

"Thinking? Do you often just sit and think? What do you think about?"

"Oh, nothing much. Here we are; this is our house."

"What a fantastic garden! Do you live with your grandparents?"

"Yes."

He stood for a moment looking at the garden, and I knew that he admired our cottage as much as I did. When he spoke again, it was almost wonderingly.

"Do you live here always? Where are your parents?"

"I haven't... well, I haven't really got any... my mother died... that's what I was thinking about. Look, there's Grandpa working on the rockery, and Gran bringing in the washing. Gran! This is Don. He's hurt his foot."

Gran hurried across the lawn, full of kindness and concern. In no time at all Don was sitting on a stool in the bathroom soaking his foot, and Gran was bustling round and organising us all.

"I think that should be stitched," she said, looking at the ugly cut. "Can we phone your father, and can he fetch you? Lucy, make a cup of tea, there's a good girl!"

"Oh yes, Dad's at home, and we've got a car," said Don, who had stopped bleeding to death. "I'll write down the number. Tell him where I am, by the big iron gates of the Estate. I'll be sitting on the garden wall waiting for him."

So Grandpa made the phone call, and Gran bandaged up the cut, and I made tea. Don soon hobbled downstairs, and ate two pieces of Gran's chocolate cake in a great hurry, because he didn't want to miss his father, and then we went out to wait on the wall in the evening sunshine.

"Thanks a lot, Lucy," he said, "I really would have been in trouble without you and your gran. And they didn't say anything about the trespassing either."

"It's not them," I replied, "it's the game-keepers. They can be really nasty. But I was thinking... suppose I took you in..."

"If I said I was a friend of yours they'd let me come, wouldn't they?" broke in Don eagerly. "I do want to dam that stream and make a big pool. How about helping me, Lucy? When my foot's better... Oh – here's my Dad!"

A car drew up sharply; the driver gave a friendly hoot and jumped out.

"What on earth, Don?" he began. "Can you walk? Where's the kind lady who rescued you?"

Gran came to the gate and said it was a pleasure but the foot ought to be stitched. Don stood grinning from ear to ear, delighted with his adventure and his dad. Grandpa joined us with a bunch of daffodils, and we all parted as good friends.

"Bye, Lucy," called Don, hobbling to the car, "I'll be seeing you!" A few moments later they were off and I watched his waving hand until it disappeared round the corner, then I slowly walked back into the house. Gran stood in the doorway looking very pleased with herself.

"Lucy," she said, "I phoned Miss Bird this afternoon. I thought you might like to get away for a little holiday over Easter. She says she can fit you into a Guide camp in Derbyshire for a week. Would you like that?"

I stared at her blankly. If she'd said this to me yesterday I should have gone crazy with excitement; but now – if I went away to camp I should never dam the stream or watch for squirrels in the early morning with Don. And if I wasn't there, he'd never be able to say he was my friend.

"I don't know, Gran," I answered slowly. "It's not as if they were girls from my school, is it? It was different sharing a tent with Mary. I wouldn't know any of these girls, would I?"

"I guess you'd know them pretty well by the end of the week," retorted Gran, "but it's up to you. We don't want to get rid of you, do we, Grandpa? I just thought the holidays were a bit lonely for you here, but maybe you could ask your friends up."

"I'm not lonely, Gran," I answered quietly. "I'd rather stay here for Easter – it's fun, and I... well, I just don't want to go away."

So I stayed and waited to see what would happen next, and four or five days later Don reappeared on a bike with his foot well bandaged. We were all having tea when he turned up, so he came in and joined us. He got on very well with my grandparents. He had never had any, he explained, because his dad had been an orphan and his mother had come from South Africa, and he seemed to take it for granted that he could share mine. He ate a great deal, and then suggested we went to look at the stream.

It was the first of several happy mornings and evenings. They were the best time to watch wildlife, he said, and anyhow, he had a job, working for his dad during the day. He was saving up for a new bike. He was always anxious to get back by 9 am, and seemed to think the hotel might collapse if he was late. But we dug out a pool big enough to wade in from the stream bed, and dammed it, and I would often hear his bicycle bell soon after sunrise. I would dress and creep down, explaining to a sorrowful Shadow that he could not come, and then we would run out and crouch in bushes to watch birds, squirrels and rabbits. Once, on a never-to-be-forgotten early morning, when we were climbing a tree and not watching at all, we suddenly saw a vixen playing with her three roly-poly cubs. They tried to bite her tail but she cuffed them on to their backs, where they lay waving their little paws in the air and rolling over each other.

Don and I didn't really talk about personal things. He told me about birds and foxes and fossils, and radar, and what his dad said and did, and I told him about the books I'd read. It was half way through the holidays before Don asked the question I dreaded, the question which always came up in the end and which I had never been able to answer. Now that I could answer, it was almost worse.

We were wandering home on a quiet, grey April evening, noticing things as usual. Don was peering round through a pair of binoculars which his dad had given him for his birthday.

"I can see that thrush right up close," he said excitedly. "I can almost count the speckles on her breast. Dad knew I wanted binoculars, and he bought me a really good pair. Lucy, what happened to your dad? Did he die too?"

Suddenly I realised that I no longer dreaded this question. I wanted to share my tangled thoughts with someone to whom I could speak quite freely without fear of hurting their feelings.

"Sit down on this log, Don," I said, "and I'll tell you all about it."

I told him everything, all about my past, and the letter, and creeping downstairs, all about Gran and Grandpa and their fears, all about the big questions that kept me awake at night, like 'when he comes, what shall I do?'

"What would you do, Don, if your dad was a wicked man in prison, and yet he wanted you?" I asked finally.

And Don, tossing back his thick brown hair from his forehead, replied without hesitation.

"I should find him, somehow, somewhere, and I should say to him, 'I don't care what you've done, Dad – I'm still your boy!'"

## Chapter Six

## Badger watching with Don and Mr Smith

We went home, and Don, after having a bun and a cup of tea, cycled away into the dusk as usual – but once again, something had happened. Somehow, through that single sentence of Don's, I suddenly knew what to do. All my confused sense of right and wrong, my wondering who to stay loyal to, seemed to have come to rest in that single sentence, as though it was a compass pointing me home. Somehow I must find my father, or wait till he found me, and tell him that, whatever he'd done, I was still his girl. For the first time I felt I was really starting out in the right direction instead of running round in circles. For the first time since I had read that letter, I fell asleep the moment my head touched the pillow.

Two days later it was Good Friday, and Gran,

Grandpa and I went to the service in the little Norman church nearby, its grey walls now surrounded by a sea of golden daffodils. I quite liked going to church; I liked wearing my best clothes and singing hymns, and I loved the musty smell and the simple beauty of the arches and pillars. During the sermon I usually made up stories while Grandpa snoozed and Gran listened. That day, though, it was a different sort of service; there was no sermon, just hymns and prayers, and I found myself listening, really listening. Then we sang a hymn I'd known since I was small, and I found myself thinking, really thinking, about the words:

"He died that we might be forgiven,

He died to make us good."

If that was true, bad people could change and even prisoners could be forgiven. While I was still thinking this out, the service ended, and we streamed out of the cool church into the green and gold of the April morning. I wondered what it was like to come out of prison... to be forgiven. I walked home very quietly, still thinking hard.

That afternoon I helped Grandpa in the garden. I felt I needed to find out everything I could from him, and besides, I liked talking to Grandpa.

"Did my mother like gardening, Grandpa?" I began.

"Well now, I don't think she did much. She loved wild, growing things, and wandering about, but she liked reading better than working in the garden. Our Alice was a great one for book learning."

"And I'm really like her, Grandpa?"

He smiled very tenderly. "You might be her all

43

over again, pretending to do a bit of weeding, and sitting back and talking instead. That was her way! It was 'Dad this', and 'Dad that'! I never got any work done when she was about."

"But aren't I like my father, Grandpa? Surely you can't be only like one parent?"

His smile faded. "I don't think you're like him at all, Lucy, and even if you are..." He paused, trying to think of the right words. "It's like this, or so it seems to me; if you cross a weak plant with a healthy plant, and then you take the seedlings and give them manure, and water them, and shelter them, and keep the slugs off them – well, they'll grow up healthy plants. The weak strain will die out. We've tried to give you plenty of sunshine and shelter, Lucy..."

"And you've kept the slugs off me," I added with a giggle. "But Grandpa, don't bad people ever turn good? I mean, don't people ever change?"

Grandpa considered this for a long time.

"Well," he said at last, leaning on his spade, "even the Bible says something about not gathering grapes from thistles. Flowers are flowers and weeds are weeds, but people *can* change, by the grace of God. But prison's a poor soil, Lucy! They mostly come out worse than they went in! But there *is* the grace of God... you'd better ask your Gran about it."

He gave a deep sigh and stooped to his seedlings, and I sighed, too, and pulled up a few more weeds, for Grandpa's answer had given me little hope or comfort. Then I glanced up, and noticed a heap of manure beside the tool shed, and gave a little cry of pleasure. Two white narcissi appeared to be springing out of it. Such beautiful flowers out of such dirty, smelly manure! I said to myself. It's like the grace of God. Ugly things *can* turn beautiful. I think bad people *can* become good.

I saw little of Don after Easter, for he had been very busy helping his father, saving up for his new bike. He had earned quite a lot of money taking luggage up in the lift, working in the garden, cleaning the car, and running errands for Mr Smith.

"Who is Mr Smith?" I asked casually. It was a warm, sleepy afternoon and we sat dangling our feet in the pool, eating our tea and exchanging news. The daffodils were nearly over, but soon the bluebells would be out.

Mr Smith, explained Don, with his mouth full, was the new man who had come to live at the hotel about ten days before. He'd taken an attic room, and was going to stay until the summer. He was a nice man, who had travelled in lots of countries – he'd been in an avalanche and seen a bullfight – but he wasn't very strong and he had a bad cough. Don liked talking to him, but wasn't allowed to disturb him much because he was always busy.

"What does he do?" I asked.

"He writes books," replied Don casually. "He's got a whole shelf of them, but he won't let me read them. He says…"

"Writes books!" I gasped. "Do you mean to say he writes real books – to be printed, and people read them?"

"Of course! What else would you do with books? Eat them?"

I gazed at Don in wonder. He ran errands for a real live author, whose books were printed! I thought of the exercise books in my bedroom, filled with pages of happy scribble; but would I ever write anything that could be printed? And who would tell me how to set about it?

"I should like to meet Mr Smith," I said boldly.

"Actually," replied Don, "he'd like to meet you. I told him how you wrote stories and poems and things, and he said he was interested in children who wrote things, and he'd like to see some of your pieces. Perhaps he'll come up to the woods with me one day when he's better, but I shan't be coming for a few days. Dad thinks there's some badgers in a little spinney off the Tewkesbury Road, and we're going there to watch. They come out when it's getting dark."

"Wish I could see them," I said.

"OK," said Don good-naturedly, "but you can't come until I know they exist. If they are really there we'll try and fix something. Badgers are worth seeing."

He was as good as his word. He came pedalling up the hill, very breathless and excited, about five days later, and burst into the kitchen where Gran and I were spending a peaceful afternoon baking for the church fête.

"Please, Mrs Ferguson," he announced, "can Lucy come? Mum says she can have tea with us at home, and then she can come and see the badgers. We saw hundreds of them, Mrs Ferguson! Well I mean, we saw at least seven! It was pitch dark and we watched them dancing and boxing."

"May I ask how, in the pitch dark?" asked Gran, smiling.

"Well, it got pitch dark as we watched,"

explained Don, "and it was pitch dark coming home in the car. When we first saw them it was sunset – the sky was all red, and we lay for ages waiting for them to come. You have to keep very, very still, Lucy. You mustn't move for about an hour."

"That must be very difficult for you!" remarked Gran, for Don could never keep still. "And who's going with you? Your father will take you, and bring Lucy back, will he?"

Don shook his head. "Dad's busy tonight," he explained, "he's got lots of guests. Mr Smith says he'll come with us. He's got a car, and he'll bring Lucy back by nine. OK, Mrs Ferguson? Oh, what fantastic cakes! Are you having a party, Mrs Ferguson?"

"Not really," smiled Gran, "but perhaps we'll have one now. Sit down, you two, and have some cake and lemonade. I want a word with Grandpa."

She was gone for quite a while, and I discovered later that she had sent Grandpa hurrying off to check up on Mr Smith from Don's parents. As he seemed to be satisfactory in every way, she returned at last and gave permission for me to go. I was wildly excited, already standing with one foot on the pedal of my bike, but whether it was because I was going to see a badger or meet a real live author, I was not quite sure.

Then we were off, speeding under the larch trees, and I remember thinking there was no joy in the world like the joy of going downhill on a bicycle with the wind singing in my ears, and my hair blowing backwards. At the bottom of the hill we skimmed into the town, and pushed our bikes across the cobbles of the old market place between the over-hanging timbered houses. Don's hotel lay at the far end, and we went round the back to his parent's flat.

"Here's Lucy, Mum," said Don abruptly, disappearing into the next room, and leaving me smiling shyly at a stout, comfortable-looking woman, who greeted me with a smile just like Don's. She told me to sit down while she finished getting tea ready. We were having it early because of the badgers, whose habits had to be timed very carefully, so I sat on the sofa while Don rushed round making preparations for the expedition. You'd have thought we were going to the North Pole from the fuss he made. Then suddenly the door opened, and a voice said quietly, "So you are Lucy, who writes poetry. Good evening, Lucy. I'm Mr Smith."

I leaped to my feet, and then tried hard not to show my disappointment. I don't know what I expected an author to look like, but certainly not like the man in the doorway – tall and thin with bowed shoulders, bald on the top of his head, and with a general look of weariness and ill-health. But I recovered myself quickly, for his face was very kind, and he looked at me with real interest. I smiled, and shook hands, and told him I was Lucy, that I did write stories and poems and things but they weren't very good.

"They'll improve if you just keep writing," said Mr Smith. "You must bring them here one day, and let me see them. I believe it's teatime now. I'm invited too, as it's a sort of badger celebration party. Let's go in together."

It really was a party, with ham and salad, fruit

and ice cream, and cake. Don's dad made all sorts of jokes and we laughed so much that it was nearing sunset when Mr Smith, Don and I finally set off in a great hurry, armed with a torch, binoculars, peppermints and a rug for Mr Smith, as he wasn't very strong. It was about twenty minutes drive through country lanes, but I hardly noticed where we were going because Mr Smith started talking to me about the books and poems I'd read, almost as though I were an equal. I found myself talking, too, as I'd never talked to any other grown-up before, until I remembered poor Don in the back, who was jigging up and down and dying to tell us all about badgers.

"They have their babies down in the setts about February," he began, when he could get a word in edgeways. "Here, this is where we stop, Mr Smith, up this little lane. You can leave the car in front of the farm, and we go across that field and through that wood, and we'll have to hide in the nettle patch; the sett is just under those bushes. You'll need that rug, Mr Smith, because of your cough..." He was hurrying across the field where the daisies were already closing their petals. As we approached the nettle patch he went down on all fours and motioned us to follow.

We crept through nettles and brambles like Red Indians stalking their quarry, until we found ourselves in a rather uncomfortable little hollow, where we crouched and tried not to scratch our nettle stings. It was rather cold and the dew was falling. I'm sure Mr Smith was longing to light a cigarette, but Don had already explained that this was absolutely forbidden as the badgers would almost certainly catch the scent, and decide to spend the evening at home.

We lay so still that we could hear all sorts of unfamiliar little sounds; the flight of wings as birds flew home, the thud of a rabbit's back legs in the field behind us. It was getting dark, and I suddenly felt glad that Mr Smith was with us. Don was leaning forward, breathless and absorbed.

And then it happened. A rustle in the dead leaves, a black nose with a gleaming white stripe – and a large badger rose up in the dusk, sniffing the air. It lolloped a few paces, and another appeared. Then they turned face to face, and rose on their hind legs in a kind of slow twilight dance; then another and another; an old fat badger, then two small, round playful cubs, tumbling about clumsily. We watched like statues till the light had gone, and there was nothing more to be seen or heard, but ghostly shapes, and queer little coughs and snufflings, and the rustling of dead leaves.

Then Mr Smith sneezed, and in one second we were alone with the chilly night, the damp ditch and the stinging nettles.

"I'm so sorry!" said Mr Smith.

"Don't worry," said Don generously. "It was too dark to see them any more in any case… Wow! I'm really aching! Weren't they fantastic, Mr Smith? Aren't you glad you came, Lucy? Bet you never saw anything as good as that before! Here, have a peppermint everybody, to warm you up! Don't step in that cowpat, Mr Smith. Race me to the gate, Lucy!"

He was in very high spirits, and chattered the whole way home, but I only half listened. I knew that I should never forget that evening as long as I lived. We had reached my gate, and the moon was flooding the garden, making Grandpa's prize tulips look like pale lanterns.

"Goodnight, Lucy," said Mr Smith, "and tomorrow write about tonight. Write about the birds flying home, and the smell of wet grass; write about what you felt when the first badger appeared... write about the moonlight on the tulips... write it all, and let me see it."

"All right," I said, jumping out of the car, "I'll try. Goodnight, and thank you very much!"

And they left me standing at the gate, wondering how he knew that was exactly what I was going to do anyway.

## Chapter Seven

# The adventure begins

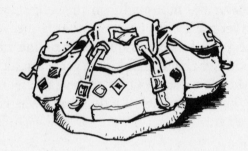

At the end of the holidays, Don and I were spending our last evening together in the bluebell wood, when Don made a disastrous suggestion to me.

We had been talking about my father again, for Don kept thinking what *he* would do if *his* dad was in prison.

"If I were you, Lucy," he remarked, "I'd run away and find him. Why don't you, Lucy? You know where the prison is. It's not very far; in fact I think it's on the main line to London. You could probably get there and back in a day if you were quick, and they couldn't stop you. All prisoners are allowed visitors. I asked my dad."

"I couldn't," I said rather crossly. "Gran would never let me. You know she wouldn't."

"You wouldn't tell her, silly," said Don. "You'd

have to say you were going somewhere else, and then not go, and then go and see your father instead. You'd probably have to make up some sort of a story, but after all, he's your father, isn't he? If it were mine, nothing would stop me!"

"But I never do go anywhere else," I objected, "and anyhow, I wouldn't have enough money, and anyhow it's wrong to tell lies, and how would I know the way?"

Don shrugged. "It could probably be worked out," he said. "Think about it, and I'll come and see you when I come home for the weekend in three weeks' time. Cheerio, Lucy! Have a good term!" He gave me a warm, hopeful smile and darted off through the arches of the wood, leaving me trying to forget this most disturbing conversation. But he had planted the seed of an idea in my mind, and neither fear, reason, nor conscience could stop it growing.

At first it was easy to forget because going back to school was always exciting and eventful, and during the first week the result of the prize essay was announced at assembly. To my amazement, I, who had never been anywhere, had won the prize. I had to walk up and receive it – a book token – and later Miss Bird read my essay aloud to the English class. I was thrilled, and so were my grandparents. I could hardly wait for Saturday to show Mr Smith.

I had started visiting Mr Smith at the weekend to show him anything I had written, and he, in his turn, gave me fresh books or poems to read. This time he seemed really pleased, and he read my essay through twice, and smiled.

"That's the way, Lucy," he said. "You really experienced this, didn't you? 'Write the things that you have seen and heard.' I believe that comes from the Bible, but I can't tell you where! What are you going to buy with your book token?"

"I don't know," I replied. "Gran said I could ask you for some ideas."

"What about a good poetry book?" said Mr Smith, after thinking for a moment. "One of these days soon I shall be going into town to buy some books myself. Do you think your grandparents would let you come with me?"

"I'm sure they would," I said enthusiastically. "I'll ask them. Thank you very much, Mr Smith, I'd love to come."

But that seed of an idea was growing and beginning to fill my mind. In the daytime I was busy with my lessons and interests, but the moment Gran had switched off the light and opened the window, my thoughts turned back to Don's suggestion and some nights I lay awake till nearly midnight, tossing, turning and planning. For now something had happened which could make the whole plan possible.

There was going to be a Whitsun camp leaving early on Whit Saturday morning. Gran would give me the money for it and would trust me to deliver it, but it would not be enough for my train fare. I had very little pocket money and my Post Office Savings book was locked away in Gran's cash-box. Also, where would I stay the night? I didn't think I would be able to manage it, so tried to forget about it once more. I put down my name for Guide camp, and asked if I could share with Mary again.

But after three weeks Don came home with easy solutions to all my problems. Money could be got somehow. He'd give me 50p himself, from his bicycle savings; in fact he produced it from his pocket and handed it over with a flourish then and there, and if I asked him, he was sure Mr Smith would buy my book token. With my own money, that ought to be enough, and the night was no problem either. He would be home for Whitsun; all I had to do was take the train to Eastbury, and go to the little spinney near the hotel and wait. He would come out every half hour and hoot like an owl, and he would put a blanket and pillow out for me in the farm barn behind the house. No one ever went there in the evening and there was plenty of straw for the horse. I could spend a comfortable night there with the horse, and wander about the hills next day until it was time to go home. He would smuggle out some food for me, and all would be well.

He was swinging on the gate as he talked. The wind blew his thick hair back from his forehead, his eyes were alight with excitement and nothing seemed impossible. And yet... I shivered with fright and misery! The spinney would be dark and lonely, and I'd never slept with a horse before. Besides, what would I say when I got home, and Gran and Grandpa asked me if I'd enjoyed camp?

Even Don admitted that this last one was the real problem!

"I think, Lucy, that you'll have to tell them," he said seriously. "After all, there's nothing all that wicked in going to see your own dad, but it's better not to tell too many lies. If you told the truth *then*, the lies you'd told *before* wouldn't matter any more, would they? And in any case, that army person..."

"Captain," I corrected.

"That Captain person might meet your Gran and tell her you hadn't been to camp, and then you'd have had it, wouldn't you!"

"I *couldn't* tell them!" I cried.

"Well," said Don patiently, "it's up to you, Lucy. I can't do any more for you. It won't be easy, admitted, but if it was my dad, I'd have a try!"

There was a fortnight to go, and I remember lying in bed at night and hearing the clock strike over and over again, waking heavy-eyed in the morning and trying to eat when I had no appetite. Whitsun was creeping nearer and nearer, and I could not make up my mind.

I had the money, or would have when Gran gave it to me for camp. Don had been most efficient in finding out when the train left and the price of a day return ticket. On the Saturday before Whitsun I had taken my book token to Mr Smith and asked him to buy it, as he needed a book himself. He had looked at me in astonishment, and I could see that he was disappointed.

"But why, Lucy?" he asked. "I thought you were going to buy that poetry book. You shouldn't sell your prize."

"I know." I felt my cheeks grow crimson. "But you see, I need the money for something very badly. Please, Mr Smith, I really do!"

"Can't you tell me what for?"

I shook my head miserably.

"Do your grandparents know?"

"Not yet... I expect they will later."

"Is it for yourself, or for someone else?"

"For someone else."

"Is it for a present?"

"Sort of... not exactly."

"Lucy, couldn't you possibly tell me?"

"Not yet... I will later. I'll come and tell you on Whit Monday, Mr Smith, honest I will... and it's nothing really naughty!"

"Does Don know?"

"Yes, and he doesn't think it's naughty either. He thinks it's something I ought to do."

"I see," said Mr Smith. He seemed to have quite a respect for Don's opinions. "Well, Don seems a good lad, and I think you're a good girl, too, so I'll trust you. And remember, on Whit Monday you're going to tell me all about it. Here's your money, but I shall keep your book token here in my drawer. You mustn't sell that; it was given you to buy books, not to sell."

Exhausted with relief, I leaned back in the armchair clutching the money in my pocket. Mr Smith started reading to me, but about ten minutes later he closed the book.

"You're not listening, Lucy," he said gently. "You're far away. I wonder what this big secret is!"

I couldn't concentrate at school, either, and my work got worse and worse. Miss Bird, meeting Gran in town one day, actually asked her if she thought I was sick. They decided between them that I was worrying about my exams, that the Guide camp would probably do me good, and that I'd better have some vitamins.

But I knew that nothing would do me good, and time was running out fast. I came home from school on Friday evening to find all that I needed for camp laid out neatly beside my rucksack: clothes, swimming things, camp money and a big bag of sweets. The sweets I would give to my father, but what on earth was I to do with all the other things? I supposed I should have to carry them round on my back until I came home again. Things were getting worse and worse.

I lay awake for a long time, trying to decide what I should say on my return. I knew the one thing Gran hated most in life was "a sly child". Only one thought kept me from giving the whole idea up, and that was that by the time I came home I should have seen my father.

I slept badly, my sleep broken by odd dreams. I had reached the prison, and my father turned away from me... I was back, coming in at the gate, but Grandpa wouldn't look up from his French beans. I woke up sweating – the birds were singing and the sun rising. No going back now! The sooner I left the better.

Dressed in my Guide uniform, with my rucksack on my back, I swallowed a hasty breakfast, and explained that I'd arranged to go to Mary's house early so that we could start together. Having started on my miserable lies, I felt I wanted to be sick. For one safe moment I clung to Gran, and the clasp of her arms was so comforting. Then I remembered that I was a "sly child" and she might never feel quite the same about me again... unless she need never know. I turned away and ran down the road without a backward look. My great adventure had begun.

Then I heard my name called urgently, and turned to see Grandpa, puffing terribly, trotting after me as fast as he could go. What could he want? I was shaking all over when he came up to me, but it was only to slip a 50p piece into my hand, unseen by Gran, who would have accused him of spoiling me. "For ice creams, Lucy," he panted, "or pop – or whatever you like. Have a good time, dearie."

It was the last straw. I snatched the money and turned away, tears streaming down my face. But no going back! There was just one more thing to be done, and then the big risks were behind me. I had written a note to Mary the night before, asking her to tell Captain that something had happened and I couldn't come to camp; I had to go somewhere else. It was a vague little note, but by the time Captain received the message I should be far away.

I crept up to Mary's front door, slipped my note through the letterbox, and darted back to the gate, but there was no escaping Mary. She saw me from the window and came bounding to the front door.

"Lucy, Lucy, wait for me!" she yelled. "Why are you running on? We were going together!"

"I can't come," I shouted desperately. "I've got to go somewhere else. Read the note, and tell Captain."

"Can't come?" squealed Mary, "Why not, Lucy? You said you'd come! And if you're going somewhere else, why have you got your Guide uniform on? Lucy, Lucy... wait..."

But I had no answer ready, and fled down the

road, with Mary, too fat to follow at my speed, shouting at me from the gate. That's done it! I thought to myself, she'll tell Captain all about me, and they'll know there's something fishy. Perhaps she'll even get in touch with Gran.

But the bus was coming, and I jumped on and reached the station. I went to the ticket-office and asked for a day return to Greening, but having never done such a thing before, I could only speak in a whisper.

"Lost your voice, love?" said the man leaning forward, and I repeated my request in a strange croak that seemed to belong to someone else.

"Over the bridge on Platform Three," said the man. "Now don't lose your ticket and enjoy your holiday!"

Down on the platform there was nearly forty minutes to wait, and I ducked behind a large litter bin in case any of my teachers were going away for the weekend. But it was all clear, and at last I actually found myself settled in a corner seat of the train, and then, for better or worse, we were off. I knew it took two and a half hours to get to Greening, but having no watch, I had no way of noticing the time. Each time the train stopped I asked the other passengers if we were at Greening.

"Relax, love," said a kind lady when this had happened four times. "I'll tell you in plenty of time to get off at Greening." And after that, I think I must have dropped off to sleep, because the next thing I knew she was shaking me gently, and we were drawing into what seemed to be an enormous station. She helped me on with the rucksack and opened the door for me. I stepped out, and joined the crowd hurrying to the exit.

## Chapter Eight

## A shock – and a mystery

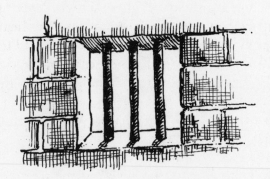

When I got outside the station and stood in the busy town street, I realised that I had no idea where to go, and dreaded asking anyone the way to the prison. They might guess my secret, or even think *I'd* done something wrong. At last I timidly asked a lady who had no idea where the prison was. Then I asked a boy, about my age, who looked friendly, but he just laughed and asked me what I'd done, and how many years I'd got.

It was well past one o'clock by now, and I was getting desperate. I'd never felt so completely alone before. I looked round and saw an old lady selling flowers, so I went over to ask her.

"Can you tell me the way to the prison?" I whispered, feeling very embarrassed.

"Prison, love?" she asked. "That's not far from

here... take the number 8 bus. It'll take you right close. Then ask again."

I ran and caught the next number 8 bus, but it was going the wrong way. I had to get off at the next stop, cross the road, and catch the next one going the right way. I realised I'd had no dinner, and was desperately hungry.

The bus conductor told me where to get off, and I hurried towards the prison at last, my heart feeling as light as air. I'd done it! I'd arrived! I thought of Don's words – "I don't care what you did, Dad." I whispered to myself "I'm your girl, and I've come."

The entrance to the prison was an enormous door in a high stone wall surrounding a yard with buildings in it, and a smaller door with a grid set in it. The bell was too high for me to reach, so I knocked hard with my fists. No one answered at first, so I went on knocking, and my heart began to beat rather fast. Supposing visiting hours were over? I started kicking rather wildly and at last the grid above my head opened and a voice said "Hello?"

"Hello," I answered, standing away from the door so that the person could see me. "I've come to see my father, Mr Martin. He's been here about nine years, and I'm Lucy Martin, his daughter."

"Sorry," said a voice, "it's not visiting day today, and children aren't let in alone. Ask your mum to bring you next time."

I could hardly believe my ears! I simply stared as the grid closed, and then I panicked. I ran at the door, kicking, hammering with my fists and shouting at the top of my voice. "Don't go away! Please,

please, don't go away; I haven't got a mother, and I've come alone... Oh, please, let me in! He's my father!"

I didn't notice the passers-by forming into a little crowd to stare at me, but one lady, who thought, no doubt, that my father had just been locked up, tried to persuade me to come away. I pushed her aside and continued banging on the door, and in the end she rang the bell above my head and the grid opened again.

"Can someone speak to this little girl?" said the lady. "She seems very upset and quite alone."

I heard footsteps going away across the court-yard, and the lady put her arm round my shivering shoulders trying to quieten me. Then we heard the sound of footsteps approaching, a key turned in a lock, and the little door set in the big door opened. A large man in a navy blue uniform stood looking down at me. "Now, now!" he said. "What's all this about?"

"It's my father," I gulped, "He's here. I came all the way from Eastbury to see him and you won't let me come in... and I don't know where to go now, and I think I've missed the last train home... and oh, please! I came all by myself... and I *must* see him. Please, please, please let me in!"

The officer looked down at me thoughtfully, and I'm sure I looked a most pitiful sight. "You'd better come inside," he said kindly; "we'll see what can be done."

I pressed through the open door without a backward look, and he led me into a small office just inside, and pointed me to a chair.

"Now," he said, "tell me all about it. What's

your name and who's your dad?"

I told him everything, feeling sure he would not refuse me. He was a patient man. He listened right through to the end without interrupting once. "And I know he's a bad man," I finished with a gulp, "or he wouldn't be here at all, but after all, he is my father... and I... I... well, we haven't seen each other for nine years and he wants me... he said so."

The warden got up and sat down at the desk. He pulled out an enormous book.

"John Martin," he murmured, turning the pages. Then he sat for a long time gazing thoughtfully down at the book, as though he didn't know what to say next.

"Your dad wasn't a bad man," he said at last. "We were all very fond of your dad... nice chap he was. But the trouble is... he's not here. He behaved so well... he got out early... left here at the beginning of April!"

For a moment I sat rigid with shock, as the real meaning of this dawned on me. Only one thing mattered. My father had been out of prison for over two months, and he'd never been near me or asked for me. It was all a terrible mistake. He didn't want me at all; I had no father. I crumpled up in the armchair, and cried as though my heart would break.

The kind warden was quite upset, but had no idea what to do. He lumbered off, scratching his head and returned with some tea and cake and a comic and told me to cheer up as he was fetching a lady who'd sort me out. I tried to sip the tea, but my tears still flowed freely, and I cried until I could cry no more. Then a lady in blue uniform arrived. She was a social worker called Miss Dixon. She acted as though she was quite used to dealing with broken-hearted children. She asked me a few questions and then said that what I needed was a meal and a good sleep, and she was going to phone my grandparents and ask them to come and fetch me. I worked myself up into quite a state when she said that, and told her I had a return ticket and could easily get myself home. I didn't want an angry Gran coming to fetch me.

"Lucy, it won't be hard to find your father. There are records kept of all prisoners and we should be able to trace him at once. But you must tell me your address, so he'll know where to find you."

I fell into the trap at once. "Pheasant Cottage, Eastwood Estate, Eastbury," I murmured, thinking that there was now no point in tracing my father. If he'd loved me, he'd have come to find me.

Miss Dixon went away and came back later saying she had phoned my grandparents and told them she was going to put me on the train back to Eastbury.

"We had a long talk," she said, "and there's nothing to be worried about. They will meet you at the station. They understand now about you wanting to see your father..."

"I don't want to see my father," I muttered, "and I'm not worried." Seeing I was about to cry again, she sensibly left me alone. I sat in silence looking at the comic until it was time to go to the station.

It was a miserable journey home, for I felt my brave adventure had failed completely. I sat dully staring out of the window until the train stopped at Eastbury and there were Gran and Grandpa hurrying forward to meet me. I noticed how white and old they looked.

I expected them to be really angry with me, but they weren't. I don't know what Miss Dixon had said to them, but Grandpa looked very miserable, and kept blowing his nose, but he spoke cheerfully, and Gran had made a special cake for tea. It was all very strange.

Don arrived after tea. He seemed rather shy at meeting Gran, so he rang his bicycle bell at the gate until I saw him and rushed out with Shadow barking a welcome at my heels. Don's eyes were nearly popping out of his head with excited curiosity.

"Whatever happened?" he began. "Didn't you go? I got the bedding over to the stable right under my mum's nose, and she never guessed, and I went to the wood and hooted about a hundred times."

"Yes, I did go," I replied. "Come up the hill and I'll tell you all about it."

He parked his bike inside the gate and we climbed the hillside to a favourite place of mine. We settled down, and I told him every detail of my great adventure.

"Bet your Gran was mad with you!" said Don.

"No, she wasn't," I replied slowly, stroking Shadow's ears. "She didn't say anything. I think Miss Dixon told her not to. But it was all for nothing, Don. He's been out over two months, and he hasn't come. I suppose he just didn't want to be bothered with me after all."

Don shook his head slowly.

"He'll come," he said. "Perhaps he's ill, or

perhaps he wants to earn some money, or find a home first, or something. I'd better go – I've got loads of homework to do."

We raced down the hill and he pedalled away, whistling. Happy Don, I thought to myself, speeding towards his beloved dad! I sighed and went into the house, glad that it was nearly bedtime.

Gran came up as usual, but she didn't tell me off. She kissed me goodnight and then lingered as though she wanted to say something but couldn't find the right words. Not like Gran at all!

"Lucy," she said at last, "I'm sorry you couldn't tell us; but never mind about that now... But I want you to understand that if your father ever turns up we will never stop him seeing you. You are free to choose."

She turned away and seemed to grope for the door, leaving me speechless and dismayed. What did it all mean? Had I been such a sly child that she did not want me any more? Had I run after a love that never existed, only to lose the strong love I already possessed? My safe little world seemed to be crumbling all round me, and I panicked. "Gran, Gran," I cried, and jumped out of bed and tiptoed downstairs to find them both. I had no idea what to say. I just had to get to them.

But on the bottom step I stopped as though turned to stone at a sound I had never heard before. Gran was crying; and between her sobs I heard her say in a broken voice, "Oh, Herbert, Herbert, whatever should we do without her?"

I turned and crept back upstairs. I had found my answer. I jumped into bed and fell deeply and peacefully asleep.

## Chapter Nine

# The most amazing day

We had a holiday on Whit Monday, and I went to see Mr Smith. I found him, as usual, bent over his writing, looking tired and worried, but he always seemed glad to see me, and always found time to share some new poem or story that he had enjoyed.

"Well, Lucy," he said, "have you come to tell me about your great secret?" He flung himself back in a comfortable chair, and I perched happily on the arm, because I had gradually come to talk openly to Mr Smith as I talked to no other grown-up.

"Well, yes," I replied, "I'll tell you now because it's all over. But I shall have to begin right at the beginning and tell you about my father. You see he did something very wicked when I was about three and he went to prison."

I glanced at him anxiously to see whether he was very shocked, but he only said, "Go on – tell me more."

So I told him my story all over again, just as I'd told Don and the warden, and, like them, he listened quietly until I had nearly finished – so quietly, with his head so bowed, that I thought perhaps he was asleep and stopped talking.

"Have you gone to sleep?" I asked softly.

He looked up quickly. "No, I'm not asleep," he said. "I'm just listening. But Lucy, tell me this. If he was such a bad man why do you want to see him again? You're happy with your grandparents. Wouldn't it be better to forget all about him?"

My eyes filled with tears. This was what I had sometimes thought myself, but Don, and my own heart, told me that my reason was wrong.

"He's my dad, isn't he?" I almost shouted. "And even if he's been bad I'm still..." I couldn't say any more, for the tears were streaming down my face. Mr Smith pulled a handkerchief out of his pocket and handed it to me, and after a few moments I was able to go on.

"I didn't forget him... I went... and it was terribly difficult... but he's forgotten me. He's been out two months now and he hasn't come... if he'd wanted me, he'd have come quick, wouldn't he?"

Mr Smith leaned forward and said quietly, "He'll come, Lucy, and he'll be a lucky man to find such a brave, faithful, loyal daughter waiting for him. You see, when people come out of prison they are sometimes ashamed and afraid. After all, from what you say, your grandparents don't seem to think much of him, do they? What would they do, if he came?"

"They... they said I could choose," I sniffed. "But they wouldn't want me to go. And... well... he was a bad man, wasn't he, to have gone to prison? And they want me to grow up good... and I couldn't leave them. I shouldn't know what to do!"

I still felt like crying, for the whole problem seemed too great to be solved and I didn't know where to turn. But Mr Smith could not tell me what to do either. He only said, "He was a bad man eight years ago, Lucy, but eight years is a long time. People sometimes change, especially when they have little daughters waiting for them. Don't worry; I think he will come in his own time, and when he comes, you'll know what to do all right."

When I got home the house was empty because my grandparents had gone to a flower show where Grandpa was showing his prize sweetpeas. Shadow came running out wagging his tail. I flung myself down on the grass and hugged him hard, for although he could not tell me what to do, he was very comforting. Gran had often told me to pray when I was in trouble, but I could never feel there was really anyone listening – like talking into a disconnected telephone.

Perhaps God did not listen because I had been so deceitful, and with my cheek pressed against Shadow's back, I made up my mind to try and be very good, to say my prayers every night, to listen in church instead of making up stories and to read the Bible even though it did not interest me. I decided to help more in the house and garden instead of always running off to play as soon as I could. I would never again tell a lie, or answer back, or pretend I had finished my homework so I could stay up later.

I tried hard to keep these good resolutions, but deep within I knew that nothing had really happened. I tried reading my Bible, but it seemed an old, dead book. In fact, church, the Bible and praying seemed like three roads that led into a thick mist, and I didn't know if there was anything beyond it.

In the meantime, the question persisted like a nagging toothache: "If my dad suddenly comes, what, oh what shall I do?"

I did well in my end of term exams, and on the first day of the holidays Mr Smith kept his promise and took me to town in his car to exchange my book token for a book. Gran had never met Mr Smith – he seemed shy of coming to the cottage – but because Don's father spoke so highly of him she let me visit him when I pleased. She saw me off at the gate after breakfast – I remember turning the corner of the road and thinking how safe and kind she looked under the arch of red roses. Neither of us had the slightest idea that this was to be the most eventful day in my whole life, and that nothing would ever be quite the same again.

It was a perfect morning. I stuck my head out of the car window and sniffed at the warm scents of summer, the new mown hay, honeysuckle and bean fields.

"Happy, Lucy?" Mr Smith asked suddenly.

I smiled and nodded. We reached the outskirts of the town and parked near the cathedral, then spent a long time in Smith's choosing my book. Then we had ice creams and visited the cathedral and when we finally came out blinking into the sunshine it was past dinner-time, so we went to the market and had ham sandwiches, custard tarts and lemonade.

In spite of the good time we were having, I couldn't help noticing how ill Mr Smith looked. He left his sandwich almost untouched and kept coughing in a nervous, worried way. By the time we reached the car he seemed to be breathing faster than usual, and as we left the town I thought he was also driving faster than usual.

"We're going home a different way," I said. "Is it quicker?"

He did not answer; he just drove faster, and after a time I noticed to my great surprise, that our hills were getting smaller and further away. Instead of driving towards them we were driving away from them.

"Mr Smith," I said, puzzled but still not alarmed, "where are we going? This isn't the way home. The hills are behind us."

But again he did not answer, and I think it was at this point that a cold trickle of fear crept into my mind, and I began to feel uneasy. Why didn't he answer? Why were we driving so fast? And why did he look so white and strange? Was I being kidnapped? Suddenly the fear broke loose and I seized his arm.

"Mr Smith," I shouted, "where are we going? I want to go home and you're going the wrong way."

He slowed up at once and drew the car on to the grass at the side of the road. For a moment we sat in tense silence, then he turned to me with that gentle smile I had come to love. I knew that I was perfectly safe with him and wondered how I could ever have been afraid.

"Lucy," he said very quietly, "do you ever still think about that bad father of yours?"

I nodded, staring. Perhaps at that moment I began to understand.

"Lucy, what would you do if he ever turned up?"

I just went on staring, and light was dawning. Old memories were stirring. Mr Smith was speaking again.

"Lucy, I'm your father... I wanted us to get to know each other better before I told you. I've written to your grandparents. Don's father took the letter up at dinnertime. I've asked them if they'll spare you for a few weeks. I want you to come away with me, if you will."

I could not speak, because the thing for which I'd been waiting, half hoping, half dreading, had happened, and it wasn't the least bit like what I'd expected. Only one thing was really clear to me – my father had come after all. He hadn't forsaken me. He'd been there all the time. I realised that I loved and trusted this man from the moment I'd set eyes on him, and now I understood why.

"Lucy," he said, "will you come with me?"

"Yes, if Gran will let me."

"But I don't think Gran will let you, or at least she'd persuade you not to. I want you to come now. I've told your grandparents in the letter that I'll phone them at half past three to talk it over. After all, I'm your father; I have the right... if you'll come."

"But I can't. I must go home first. I haven't got

my pyjamas and toothbrush or anything."

"We'll buy all you need in the next town. Will you come?"

"But I can't. I haven't said goodbye to Gran and Grandpa."

"But if we go back you won't come at all. You could say goodbye on the phone. Tell them you want to go just for a few weeks. I've promised faithfully to bring you back before school."

"But I can't. They'd be so sad; and Gran would be so cross."

"I'm not sure that they'll be either now that they've read my letter. They knew it was coming, and I think they may be relieved that I want you to stay with them during term-time. They've been so good to you and that's a good school you go to – you must finish there. I only want you for a holiday at present, and I could have asked for you altogether. But of course it is really up to you. We can say goodbye on the phone and go straight on or, if you decide against it, we'll turn back. I can drop you near the gate and go on. My luggage is in the boot, and I'm leaving today."

"But why won't you come in and talk?"

"Because your gran said long ago that she never wanted to see me again. And if we talk you'll give in and stay. You couldn't stand up to them... they've brought you up too well. So it's now or never. Will you come?"

I was silent, and I knew he was watching me as though his life depended on it. This was the moment I'd dreaded, and I felt torn in half. Pictures seemed to flash on the screen of my mind, little forgotten scenes, all crystal clear – Gran waiting at the bus stop as I came out of primary school, Grandpa leaning over the gate peering into the dusk for my homecoming, Shadow prancing down the path... They seemed to be drawing me back to the old, secure, obedient life. I looked up imploringly and shook my head.

And then at last a scene, clearer than all the others. Don, standing among the daffodils with his head thrown back, his hazel eyes very bright, his voice challenging me: "I should find him somewhere somehow, and I should say to him, "'I don't care what you've done, Dad. I'm still your boy.'"

I drew a deep breath and nodded.

"I'll come," I whispered, "when I've phoned Gran and Grandpa."

His tired face relaxed. "Thank you, Lucy," he said. "There's a hotel in the next town and we'll phone from there." We drove on in silence and I leaned my spinning head against his shoulder, and tried to take in that this was my father. We stopped at an inn called the 'Cat and Compasses' and he ordered tea for me while he went to phone. He was away a long time but when he came back he looked brighter. "Come quick," he said, "I've left the receiver off for you."

I was not very used to talking on phones and I hardly knew what to say. "Gran, Grandpa," I cried, "Do you mind? Please say I can go! You see, he was my father all the time... Gran, Grandpa – it's only for a few weeks. I'm coming back for sure, and I'll write to you every day."

"Lucy, Lucy!" It was Gran's voice urgent and pleading. "Do you really want to go? He won't take you against your wishes. Just tell him."

"But Gran, I must go. You see, he's my father, and he's not a bad man. It was all a mistake and he's a good man now. We must give him a chance, mustn't we? Grandpa..."

"God keep you, my darling child!" It was Grandpa's voice, distressed but firm. "Don't worry about us, Lucy. It had to come. Only write often and come back. Now goodbye!"

"Goodbye, Gran; goodbye, Grandpa. Write to me; kiss Shadow and tell Don." I was frantically kissing the phone, but my father took it gently from me and laid it down.

"I think that's enough," he said. "They understand, and they're glad it's only for a holiday. Now we must be on our way."

I jumped into the car and we were off, and my heart was in a turmoil of sorrow, relief, regret, excitement, and a wild sense of freedom. The hills were behind us now, and there was no turning back.

In front of us the road rose to a bright horizon, and beyond that...? I suddenly began to wonder and turned towards him.

"Mr Smith... I mean, Daddy... where are we going?"

"To London tonight," he replied. "And tomorrow we must take your photograph, and finish off your passport. We are flying to the south of Spain. I've got your ticket in my pocket. You'll be able to swim in the blue Mediterranean, and we'll stay with your old nurse. She's longing to see you."

But once again I was struck speechless. The day after tomorrow I was going to see the sea!

## Chapter Ten

# Spain – and important conversations

Two days later I stood completely dazed and bewildered in the hot foreign airport, marvelling at the speed of the Spanish language that was being spoken all round me. Out of the window of the plane I had seen the sea, and as soon as my father had collected the luggage we were going to travel by bus along the coast, and I should see it to my heart's content, and tomorrow I should swim in it!

We jumped into the two last seats of the bus and rattled off towards the town, and I sat silent, trying to take in all the new sights and sounds of Spain. The hills and palm trees were silhouetted black against the rosy colours of the sunset sky, and in the east shone the thin silver horizon where the sun still touched the sea.

By the time we transferred our luggage to

another bus, and started our journey south, it was almost dark, but the darker it grew, the livelier the streets became. We kept rattling through colourful little coastal towns, where people ate and drank, and danced, and played guitars and sold souvenirs on the pavements. After about an hour, the bus drew up in a cobbled square, and my father said, "Come on, Lucy. Here we are."

We gathered up our luggage, and pushed our way through the jostling streets until we came to a long, low house a little way out of town. It was a sort of bar, and once again people sat all over the pavement laughing, and eating shrimps and olives, and drinking wine. We went round to a door at the side, and my father knocked.

It was opened instantly, and a voice cried "Lucita, Lucita," followed by lots of Spanish. A woman had thrown her arms round me, was holding me close and kissing me over and over again, and somehow the clasp of her arms and the sound of her voice seemed familiar. We had somehow all got in the kitchen, and she was holding me at arm's length, half laughing, half crying, and a pretty dark-haired girl was stroking my hair and smiling shyly. Three more dark-eyed little children were pressing round us. My father laughed.

"Don't look so surprised, Lucy," he said. "This is your old nurse, Lola, and this is Rosita who was born the same month as you; you shared her cot! And this is Pepito, who was a fat baby when I last saw him... the others I don't know yet, but you'll soon learn to understand them."

"Pedro, Conchita," said Lola proudly, pushing them forward, "and Francisco," she added, pulling a sleepy, blinking baby out of a crib and holding him up. Then she dumped him in Rosita's arms and turned to my father, laughing, and waving her hands about, and to my great surprise he appeared to understand, and spoke back to her in Spanish.

The whole family escorted us to two white-washed rooms at the back of the house opening onto a courtyard with a great vine growing over-head. A low table in the middle of it was set for supper, which was brought in by the whole family – potato omelettes, bottles of wine, Spanish paella and great red slices of water melon. The heat and the smell of oil were making me feel quite dizzy, so Lola helped me into bed. Before I lay down I opened the window that looked out on to the beach, and heard the sound of small waves break-ing and drawing back over pebbles. Tomorrow... tomorrow...

The sun streaming into the room and the cries of the fishermen woke me early next morning, and I rushed to the window and breathed in the salty, fishy air and watched them pulling in the nets and excitedly sort the catch. To me it was as fascinat-ing as a play, and I think I would have stayed there for hours watching the sparkling sea and the busy beach if Rosita had not put her head round the door and signalled for me to follow her.

I soon got ready. My father was still asleep, and a singing girl was cleaning the little bar. I was daz-zled by the bright early sunlight in the streets and the colours of the little town. Wherever we went, Rosita introduced me proudly as her friend – "*Lucita – mi amiga.*"

It was the first of many happy mornings, for life

in Spain followed a happy pattern. Lola and Rosita kept very busy running the inn as well as doing all the household chores. I helped where I could, while my father got on with his writing. I had my meals with him at the table under the vine. He often looked weary and ill after a morning's writing and seemed out of breath, but he was always gentle and glad of my company, and we talked for ages about all sorts of things. Only one subject we had never touched on, and I used to think it came between us, until one afternoon we suddenly found ourselves talking about it.

"Daddy," I said, "did Mummy know Lola and Rosita?"

He nodded.

"They were great friends, and both expecting their first babies at the same time. I was brought up in Spain, and I thought there was nowhere like it. I wanted your mother to love it too, and we kept a successful little guest house just across the street. When you were born, and she died, Lola fed you and brought you up with Rosita. I gave up the business, came here to this room as a paying guest, and tried to get on with my writing. But I think I stopped caring about anything, except you, and I didn't write much."

"But why didn't you go to Gran and Grandpa's?"

"I wasn't the sort of man they wanted for their daughter, Lucy, and when she married me secretly, against their wishes, they more or less cut me off. Alice planned to take you home on a visit – she was sure it would all blow over then. She hated to be on bad terms with anyone, and, sure enough, when she died they tried hard to get in touch. But at that point I suppose I cut them off. I only knew one thing clearly then, and that was that I wanted to keep you by me. You're very like her, Lucy, and I always wished I'd known her as a child, and could have watched her grow up."

"And then?"

"How much have your grandparents told you?"

"Only what I told you. I asked Grandpa and he didn't know much – just about some drugs... and that you went to prison."

"Right! I'll tell you everything. I met a drug dealer by chance in a café, although I think now that he'd been following me for some time. I was just the man he wanted. I'd lived in Spain for years, knew the language, needed money badly, and was half crazy with grief. At first it all seemed quite small, but by the time I realised what a big affair it was, it was too late to pull out. They can get very nasty with people who turn against them. Besides, in a way, I was quite enjoying it!"

"But why did you enjoy it, when it was so wrong?"

He looked rather sad.

"I didn't think about it being wrong then. I was so lonely without your mother I just wanted something to make me forget, I didn't care very much what. Smuggling was dangerous and exciting, and I didn't stop to think about what I was handling. It brought me lots of money too. I bought a car for myself, and things for you and Rosita." He smiled, and lit another cigarette.

"And then?"

"Well, it all got bigger and bigger until I realised

I was involved in a huge international heroin ring. And by then, as I said, it was too late to get out. I did it for three years, taking bigger and bigger risks. My big mistake was going to England to meet a contact. The police were waiting for me at the airport and that was that. I'm glad I wasn't taken in Spain, or I might never have been allowed back."

"And then you went to prison?"

"Well, they let me settle you up with your grand-parents first, and then, yes, I was sent to prison for ten years, but they cut it down to eight."

"Well," I said thoughtfully, "I don't think it was all that bad. I mean, it's not as bad as stealing or killing people, is it?"

My father became very serious.

"Lucy," he said, "to start someone taking drugs is far, far worse than killing him outright. I soon realised that when I got to prison and had time to think. Never, never have anything to do with it."

"Then were you very sorry in prison? Wasn't it very nasty?"

"Well, I don't know. You mustn't think prisons in England are cruel places. I spent a lot of time in the infirmary where I was very well treated indeed. But the evenings were pretty bad, locked in those cells, with nothing to do but think. Fortunately I had my writing. I had plenty to write about by that time. What really made me sorry was missing you growing up, and all through my own stupid fault."

"But weren't you ever sorry because... well, sort of... because of God?"

"God, Lucy? Believe in God if you like, but he never did much for me except take my wife. No, I was sorry about the lives I'd helped to ruin, and I wanted to be different because of you. You're all I've got now. Old friends kind of disappear when you come out of prison; there's only you."

"But why didn't anyone tell me? Then I could have come and seen you?"

"I agreed with your grandparents that it was far better for you not to know while you were little. It's no fun having a father in prison whom you're ashamed of. Children ask questions. You'd never have felt safe."

"But why didn't you tell us it was you when you came out?"

"Because I wanted to introduce myself and get to know you in my own way. If your grandparents had known they'd have turned you right against me, wouldn't they... you know they would."

His voice was hard and bitter, and I was rather uneasy because Gran would have considered this shocking talk, but somehow talking to Dad was quite different from talking to Gran, or even Grandpa. Gran knew all the answers, and always told me what I ought to think about everything, and if I happened to think differently then I was wrong, and it had always seemed very peaceful and safe.

But this man with his sad, questioning eyes and wounded past did not know all the answers and he wanted me to think and find out for myself.

Our talk was interrupted by an excited knocking on the door, and Pepito burst in with a letter.

"Lucita!" he shouted and thrust it at me. It was my second letter from my grandparents, and a rush of homesickness came over me as I took it, as though they were stretching out steadying hands across the miles. I stood up. "I'm going under the trees opposite to read my letter," I said, and Dad smiled and nodded. I had discovered a farm, an old stone cross and a plantation of olive trees. This was the shadiest place I knew, and I made towards it clutching my precious letter.

People who lived near the inn were beginning to know me, and I had already picked up a few words of Spanish and enjoyed greeting people in the friendly Spanish way. But today the neighbourhood was very quiet and only one old woman, dressed in black, sat at the door of her house with a tortoiseshell cat beside her.

Something about her reminded me of Gran. For the first time since arriving in Spain I felt really homesick. I turned to the old woman and found her looking at me kindly. I was strangely attracted, and when she moved up, I sat down on the step beside her and stroked the cat. This pleased her, and she turned and opened the door of the house and pointed to a basket of kittens under the table.

I went to play with them for a few minutes, and as I did so I looked round. It was very bare and very clean; just a bed, a rush mat, a table and chair, a box and on it a big black book that looked like Gran's family Bible. I looked at it more closely. It *was* a Bible – the words *La Biblia* were engraved in gold on the cover. So this old woman believed in God, and if what Gran said was true, God was the only person who could help me choose whose side to take.

I said goodbye to the old woman, and she stroked my hair, and made signs to me to come again. I nodded, and trotted off along the dirt track to the olive trees and began to read my letter.

They had both written. Gran's letter was full of good advice. "We pray for you every day," it ended, "and ask God to take care of you. Say your prayers every night and trust in your heavenly father." Grandpa's letter was full of anxious love, and news about the marrows and Shadow, the cat and the church fête, all the little bits of home that I wanted to hear. I sat for a long time reading and re-reading my letters, and I finally turned back to the end of Gran's. "Say your prayers every night, and trust your heavenly father..." "God? Believe in God if you like, Lucy, but he's never done anything for me except take my wife!" Oh, who was right and how could I find out? Would that dull old book tell me anything I wanted to know? I would try again, for I felt torn in half, and I really needed to know, for the great question was still unresolved. Who was I really going to belong to?

Today was Friday. Only two days till Sunday, and then we would all go to church. Maybe I would find my answer then.

## Chapter Eleven

## I find an answer

We spent most of Saturday on the beach, swimming and playing round the boats and rock pools. In the afternoon my father walked along the coast with us to a lonely bay with white sand, where we looked for shells. I lay on the hot rocks and gazed into a pool like a miniature garden, with starfish, sea anemones, waving seaweeds and tiny whelks. I thought God must be a wonderful Creator to design such fragile beauty.

On Sunday we were having breakfast in our little patio and the church bells were pealing out all over the town.

"Daddy," I said firmly, "it's Sunday. Can I go to church like I do at home, and can I have a Bible to read?"

"I'm afraid I haven't got a Bible," he said, "and

as the churches in this town are all in Spanish, you wouldn't understand a word. Besides, they're not the kind of churches you've been used to." He hesitated, as though he had more to say.

"Lucy," he said at last, "I want you to tell me this; why do you want to go to church? Does it mean anything to you at all? Do you just go because Gran tells you to? And do you read your Bible because it helps you or makes a difference to you? Or is it because you've been taught it's the right thing to do? Think it out and give me an answer. I really want to know. I don't like people who just pretend to be good or religious, and I don't want you to be one."

I stared at him. I knew none of the answers I could have given would satisfy him.

Lola and the other children had gone to Mass in their best Sunday clothes, and the bells had stopped ringing. My father seemed more breathless than usual, and I hadn't the heart to ask him to come to the beach, so I sat beside him and wrote to Gran, then I went down to the beach to look for shells by myself.

We were invited to dinner in the inn kitchen where we gathered round the table under sides of bacon and bunches of herbs and garlic hanging from the ceiling. Several bottles of wine were drunk and everyone became very happy and talkative. By the time we had finished it was late in the afternoon. Sunday was hurrying past, and I had still found no answer to Dad's question, nor any solution to my problem. For the first time I felt really lonely, and I thought of the old woman up the hill. I would go and visit her.

"Daddy," I said, "I'm going to visit an old woman who lives just the other side of those eucalyptus trees. Can I take her one of our peaches?"

"Take her two, Lucy." He picked out the best and put them in a bag. "I'm glad you're making friends round here; you'll be chattering Spanish in no time, and I want you to love Spain. Don't go far, and come back before sunset."

I slipped out quietly in case the other children saw me and wanted to come with me. I liked being with them, and I loved Rosita, my *amiga,* but now I wanted to be alone. It was still very hot, and I was glad of the shade of the eucalyptus trees. I liked their smell, the rustle of their dry leaves and the whirring sound of the cicadas who made such a noise, but whom I could never see.

I walked slowly, thinking about Dad's question. What did church really mean to me? I thought of Sunday at home – putting on my best clothes, singing the hymns as loudly as I could; making up stories and poems during the sermon and hoping it wouldn't be too long; Grandpa falling asleep and Gran looking at us out of the corner of her eye; the prospect of a roast Sunday dinner, my favourite pudding and a free afternoon... Did church really mean anything more? I couldn't honestly say that it did, except very occasionally, like on Good Friday or Easter Day.

When I came to the house at the edge of the vineyards there was no one to be seen. They were probably all still having a siesta and would come to life at sundown. So I knocked rather timidly at the old woman's door, but it was opened immediately by her little granddaughter. I peeped in, and there was my friend sitting at the table, her glasses on her nose, reading her Bible.

Why? What did it mean to her? Something, I was sure, judging from the look on her face. As I couldn't speak to her, I did a strange thing. I went straight up to her and put the peaches on the table. Then I pointed to the book and repeated the word that the children at the inn said about a hundred times a day: *"Por que..."* "Why?"

She did not seem at all surprised. She just pointed to a word on the page, and I squatted down beside her to look. "Jesus." It was the same in English as it was in Spanish. She repeated it, and then, pointing upwards, she said very simply, *"Jesus es mi amigo."*

*Amigo* – it was the word Rosita used when we walked down the road arm-in-arm and she introduced me to everybody. *Mi amiga*, because I was a girl, but the same word. "My friend... Jesus, my friend..." – not someone in history, but near and alive. I suddenly realised as I gazed at the page that praying and Bible reading and church-going were no longer three roads leading into the mist. The mist was clearing, and the roads were leading to a bright centre. They led to Jesus – not a person in a book who died hundreds of years ago, but someone who was alive now. He was the old woman's friend, and I saw no reason why he shouldn't be my friend, too. For I suddenly knew that this was what I had been looking for all the time... not words, or rules, but a person.

The discovery was so great that I can't quite remember what happened next. I wanted to stay near this old woman whose friend was Jesus, but we couldn't find any more words in common. Somehow I found myself on the dirt track that led to the farm, and there in front of me was the stone cross, which now seemed very important, because it was on a cross that my friend Jesus had died.

"Thank you," I said, looking up at it, and at that moment I knew what saying my prayers really meant. It was just talking to my friend, saying thank you, telling him things and knowing that he was listening. It was too hot to stay long near the cross, but I sat under an olive tree nearby and stared across at it and started to talk to him. I asked him never to let me tell lies again, and I asked him to show me how to choose, and to make my grandparents and my father like each other so that we could all be one family.

The stone cross cast a long shadow along the path, and in my imagination the dirt track, lit up in the mellow light of the sunset, seemed like the beginning of a new life. I could set out on this bright road with all my tangled, troubled past behind me, and Jesus, my friend, beside me. I loved him, and longed for a Bible, because it no longer seemed a dull old history book, but a book where I could learn more about my friend.

The sun disappeared as I came out through the eucalyptus wood, and the sky was streaked with crimson. Lights were coming on in the shops, and the town was waking up. My father was sitting at a table on the pavement having a drink. I sat down beside him, happy, hot and thirsty, and he ordered me a lemonade.

"Daddy," I said eagerly, "you know what you asked me?"

"When Lucy?"

"This morning – about church and the Bible."

"Oh, yes! Have you thought about it?"

"Yes, and I know the answer. The old woman told me."

"What? In Spanish?"

"Yes, and I understood. I know now!"

"Really? Do tell me!"

"I want to go to church, and I want to read my Bible, because... because Jesus is my friend."

I expected him to smile that twisty smile of his, but he didn't. He just looked at me, and then replied very gently, "In that case, Lucy, I'll get hold of a Bible for you as soon as I can, and if there's such a thing here, and if you're happy to go on your own, I'll find an English church service for you."

## Chapter Twelve

# A trip to Gibraltar

Waking up next morning, everything seemed the same as usual; the patch of sunlight on the wall, the lap of waves on the pebbles, the shouts of the fisherman. But then I remembered that everything was different – I was no longer a troubled child, pulled in two directions, not knowing what to believe or where to turn.

My father looked very tired and pale at breakfast and coughed a lot. But he seemed cheerful, and suggested we took a bus down the coast to the southernmost tip of Spain, where I could see the Rock of Gibraltar and the coast of North Africa, and I could have a swim. I was thrilled, for I loved doing things with my father. He was such good company and knew so much about everything. I seized my costume and we went to the bus stop and bought a picnic in the market while we waited.

I shall never forget that day, and yet I didn't know at the time that it was a very special day, because nothing very special happened. We were just happy together. The bus rolled along the coast road with the sea on one side and the vineyards and olive groves on the other and sometimes a field of sunflowers facing east. No one could tell stories like my father, and he kept me spellbound telling me about the Spanish civil war until the rattling bus lurched round a corner and I gave a gasp. There in front of me lay the sapphire blue Straits of Gibraltar and the Rock, like a grand old lion sitting in the sea. Across the Straits, misty but visible, were the high mountains of the North African coast. As the bus rattled into town, Dad started telling me about the habits of the Rock Apes of Gibraltar and the snake charmers of Tangier.

It was very, very hot down in the town, so we stopped for ice creams outside a little café where about half the customers had darker skin and talked Arabic instead of Spanish. Then we looked at the shops and I spent a long time choosing presents for Gran and Grandpa. My father sat on a chair in the shop, smoking and half-asleep, and did not hurry me at all.

Then we sauntered along the water's edge to the beach and I slipped into my costume and raced towards the sea, dashing into the small waves, falling headlong, and striking out towards the deep water. I thought that first cool plunge was the most wonderful feeling on earth.

"Don't go too far," shouted my father, and I

turned and swam back towards him. I wished he would come in too, but he didn't seem to have the energy. When at last I finished swimming, he had found a shady corner and unpacked the picnic, and I flung myself down beside him, feeling so happy and glad to be alive.

"Tell me more about that old woman yesterday," said my father suddenly. "She interests me."

I looked up eagerly.

"She's a nice old woman. She lives in a tiny house on the other side of the eucalyptus trees. She's got a cat and a goat and a whole basket of kittens and a little granddaughter and a Bible, and I've visited her twice."

"But how do you communicate? Surely she doesn't know English?"

"Oh no; but I told you, she's got a Bible and we read it together. She pointed to the word '*Jesus*' and it's the same word in English and Spanish."

"I see! And what happened next?"

"She said Jesus was her *Amigo* and I know that word, too. Rosita calls me her *amiga*. It means friend."

"Go on," said my father, "tell me more."

I munched my sandwich thoughtfully.

"Well," I began rather shyly, "I wanted him to be my friend too. So I went to the cross..."

"The cross? What do you mean?"

"Along the path by the vineyards. There's a farm with a little white pig loose outside and some hens, and near the gate there's a stone cross. And I sat there until I was too hot, and then I sat under a tree."

"And what did you do under the tree?"

"Well... I said sorry; and then... well, I said thank you. And after that... well, I asked him to be my friend too."

"And what happened?"

"Well, I walked home. The cross was behind me, and everything in front was sort of shining from the sunset. And I was happy, because now I've got a friend and I can tell him all my troubles."

"Your troubles, Lucy? I should like to know your troubles too. What are they?"

I turned and faced him steadily.

"I asked him to make you and Gran and Grandpa like each other, so we can all be one family," I said. "That's my biggest trouble. It's horrible having to choose. Can I have a banana, please?"

He did not ask any more questions. He lay back on the sand and closed his eyes, and I thought he was asleep. Only when I got up to run back in the sea did he speak.

"The time's getting on," he said. "Run and have a last swim and then we must get back."

We got on the bus in the cobbled square; I sensed that my father was very tired, and we travelled home almost in silence. I leaned my head against his shoulder, and gazed for the last time at the Rock, the Straits and the North African ranges across the sea. Then the bus swung round a corner and they were gone.

My father went straight to bed when we got home, and I went into the kitchen and sat with Rosita under some dried fish hanging from a beam and ate a tortilla. There was great excitement because Lola's brother had come from Barcelona and brought a little rubber boat that you could blow up and float on the waves. Pepito and Pedro just couldn't wait for the next morning. Their uncle was a large man with shiny black hair who laughed a lot and drank a lot, and we all got very warm and merry. It was quite late when I left them, still celebrating, and slipped into our own apartment. The moon was shining right over the patio, and I could hear my father's rather fast breathing. I tried to tiptoe in without waking him, but he called to me.

I'd kissed him goodnight and was leaving the room when he spoke again.

"Lucy," he said, "if what that old woman told you makes you happy, hang on to it. That sort of thing cheered your mother up when she was expecting you... you may need it... one of these days..."

I asked him to explain, but he said it was time to sleep. I climbed into bed and lay awake for a long time watching the moonlight on the white wall and wondering what he meant.

## Chapter Thirteen

# An unforgettable day

Next day Pedro and Pepito came knocking at our door in a great state of excitement, inviting me to join them and the uncle from Barcelona. He was taking the rubber boat down to the sea, and they were all taking a picnic to the little lonely beach with white sands, and were leaving right away.

I hesitated. I wanted to go, but it would mean leaving my father for hours. "Couldn't you come too, Daddy?" I asked.

"Not now," he replied. "I must do some writing this morning, but I may stroll along and join you after lunch."

So we all set off in our swimming things, dancing along at the edge of the waves. The uncle from Barcelona kept the children in fits of laughter with his jokes and stories, but as I couldn't understand what he was saying I tripped along in front, enjoying the beach with its smells and sounds. I walked slowly, looking for shells and running in and out of the water and wishing this walk could last forever. But it was not so far after all, and we reached our special bay long before dinner-time.

The rubber boat was a great success, and we all had rides in turns, with Uncle splashing along behind like an enormous porpoise. Pedro and Pepito loved it, and climbed in and out at least fifty times. Then, exhausted with swimming, laughing and shouting, we pulled the boat on to the beach and settled down to our picnic – bread, olives, sardines, gherkins and tomatoes, followed by slice after slice of water melon.

Uncle made his way towards a beach café for a drink. He said he wouldn't be long, and until he came back no one was to go into the sea or play with the boat.

Rosita, Pedro and Pepito nodded vigorously, but Concha was not listening; she sat with her back to us, busy making a sandcastle, and no one took any notice of her.

Uncle left us, and Rosita and I searched for treasures in the rock pools, while the boys went off to roll down the sand dunes. It was very peaceful in this small bay, and being lunchtime we were the only people there.

Suddenly, Pedro and Pepito started screaming – loud, raucous screams that shocked the sleepy silence. Rosita and I whirled round to see them running across the sand, pointing and screaming.

Pointing at what? We turned and saw. Some way out to sea the rubber boat bobbed on the sparkling water, and in it sat Concha, quite enjoying the ride.

We all ran and screamed and hurled ourselves in the sea, but Rosita realised at once that we could never reach her, and the boat, carried by the wind, was moving out to sea much quicker than we could swim, tipping dangerously. She hauled in her brothers and gave frantic directions. They were to run like the wind to the café and fetch Uncle, and I was to run like the wind in the opposite direction, to where we had seen the fishermen painting their boats and mending their nets. She would stay and watch in case Concha got frightened and fell into the sea.

Never before had I run as I ran that day, unseeing, blinded with horror, for it was all our fault. And how would I explain in Spanish? And would they still be there, and would they come? Concha was only a baby. Supposing when we got back there was just an empty boat bobbing on the waves. "Please, please, God!" I cried as I sped across the sand, and suddenly remembered he was not far away at all. He was the friend close beside me who had once walked on the waves. He could still walk on the waves and reach that bobbing little boat with the precious baby in.

"Lucy, Lucy, are you practising for the Olympics?"

With great relief I realised that I'd bumped into my father strolling along to join us. I flung my arms round his waist, too breathless to speak, looked up at him and pointed backwards.

He saw by my expression that something was seriously wrong, and shaded his eyes to see where

I was pointing. Then he shouted "Go and fetch those fishermen behind the rock, and a boat," and, pushing me away from him, he began to run as I'd never dreamed he could run.

Exhausted and panting, I somehow managed to stumble on and found the two fishermen stretched out asleep on the sand in the shade of their boat. I jumped on them and shook them, and they sprang up, swearing fiercely in Spanish, but somehow I managed to let them know that I was in trouble and persuaded them to come and see. As soon as we came in sight of the little rubber boat we realised that help was no longer needed. It had already arrived.

My father had reached the boat and was swimming slowly back, propelling it with his hand, while Concha sat smiling and enjoying her little trip. Uncle and the boys had just arrived with a great many other people, all talking excitedly. Only Rosita stood tense and rigid, her black eyes looking enormous in her white face. I ran to comfort her but she did not seem to notice me.

Soon they were in shallow water, and my father gave the boat a little shove. It was carried in on the breaking waves, and Concha came running in through the spray straight into the arms of Rosita, who had hysterics and sank down on the beach laughing and crying and clasping her frightened little sister.

Everyone pushed and jostled round the children, and no one, except me, turned to welcome the man walking in from the sea.

How slowly he walked! He seemed to be staring at me without seeing me and his face was a strange, blue-grey colour. I ran into the water and held out my hands, and he reached blindly towards me and stumbled. Then he swayed and fell face downward on the sand, taking great, gasping breaths.

He was instantly surrounded by the noisy, excited crowd, and for a time I could not see what was happening. I think one of the fishermen was trying to do artificial respiration, and Uncle was running up the beach. I heard the words "policia" and "ambulancia" repeated many times, and more and more people arrived. I tried to push my way through the crowd, but I was held back, for they needed room at the centre. Then the noise died away, and quietness seemed to gather round the still figure in the centre. People began shaking their heads, and sighing deeply. At last we heard the siren wail of the ambulance, and some men in uniform came running down the beach, followed by two policemen.

My father was carried away on a stretcher. I struggled loose from the crowd and ran after them, pleading to be allowed to go with him, but the door was slammed in my face and he was taken away.

We wandered home in a sorry procession. Rosita walked beside me, loving and consoling, but I shook my head and refused to be comforted.

When we reached the inn, the children poured out the story to Lola, who wept and scolded Concha and hugged her, and scolded the family and wept some more. But when she heard about my father she dumped Concha on the bed and folded me in her arms. Then she sent her brother immediately to the hospital to ask for news.

He was away a long time, and we sat huddled in the kitchen. Rosita would not take her eyes off Concha. Lola tried to tempt me to eat, but I could do nothing but wait anxiously. At last we heard fast, heavy footsteps in the street and Uncle came in and they all gathered round him and started talking very fast while I watched their faces and gathered that my father was still alive. Then Lola threw a shawl over her head, held out her hand to me and pointed up the hill, so I supposed we were going to the hospital.

We twisted our way up many sloping, cobbled streets before we reached its iron gates. An old nun let us in and she and Lola talked rapidly in low voices while I sat on a bench. The afternoon sun was shut out and I gazed round the cool corridor and wondered where my father was, and what he looked like now. Opposite me on the wall hung a crucifix – not a stone cross like the one by the farm, but a cross with a figure on it.

I suddenly remembered that the crucifixion was something that had happened nearly two thousand years ago; it was all over, and death had not been the end. Jesus had come back, and was alive, and strong, and able to help me. I turned my face away from the figure on the cross and thought of my father, that last desperate swim, and little Concha safe and alive and singing in the kitchen, while Daddy had nearly died instead. He'd got there just in time to save her. Perhaps if I could see him and tell him, he'd understand.

The nun came over to me. She was a gentle old woman, and thankfully she knew a few words of

English.

"Your father," she said, "very ill... bad heart... come, but no much talk!" She laid her fingers on her lips, and I followed her up a staircase and into a small private ward where my father sat in bed, propped upright with pillows. He had a rubber tube in each nostril attached to a cylinder. His face was still a strange colour, but the loud breathing had stopped and his eyes were open, and fixed on me. I kissed him very gently and sat down as close as possible beside him. The nun waited by the door.

"Lucy, darling," my father spoke in a whisper, and his words came haltingly, "are you all right?"

"Yes, Daddy; are you? You're better, aren't you?"

"A little; is Lola here?"

"Yes, she's downstairs. Shall I fetch her?"

"In a minute... stay a little longer... then I want to tell her to send a telegram to your grandfather... He must come at once..."

My face lit up.

"And when he comes, will you see him and talk to him?"

"Yes... yes... I want to talk to him. Is Concha all right?"

"Yes, quite all right... she's singing and they're all so glad she's alive." I hesitated, not quite knowing how to say what I so much wanted to say. "Daddy, you nearly died, didn't you, so that Concha would be rescued and not drown... and Daddy, I was thinking, it was rather like Jesus on the cross, wasn't it, dying instead of us, to save us. If you hadn't swum out and nearly died, she'd have been carried right away or fallen out... you got there just in time, didn't you?"

He closed his eyes and the nun came forward and laid her hand on my shoulder.

"Little girl, come," she said. "Your father very ill so you go now. Tomorrow he better. Tomorrow come."

But she waited while I kissed him and he held my hand in both his own and opened his eyes again.

"Yes, just in time," he whispered. "Wasn't it a good thing, Lucy, that I got there just in time?"

## Chapter Fourteen

## "Jesus in my heart"

The next day seemed very long, and I wasn't allowed to see my father until 5.00 pm. I was not very worried about him because he had come round, and I thought he would just carry on getting better. Also the nun had said "Tomorrow he better", and she ought to know, if anyone did.

Besides, if it hadn't been for his illness, my prayer would never have been answered. Now all that I longed for was going to happen. Grandpa was coming – at least I was pretty sure it would be Grandpa for he would not want Gran to come alone, and one of them would have to stay with the chickens. He and my father would talk and be friends – I was quite sure of that. Everyone liked Grandpa, and he would see at once that Daddy was a good man now. How could he think anything else when Daddy had nearly died saving Concha? And then, of course, Daddy would come back to Pheasant Cottage when he was better and we'd all be one happy family at last!

The time seemed to pass very slowly while we waited for the reply to the telegram. It was so lonely in our apartment without Daddy and I longed for someone to talk to. I suddenly remembered the old woman. I'd never been to tell her what happened, and I knew she'd be interested. I waited until siesta time and then I slipped out, and crossed the main road into the shade of the eucalyptus trees.

I had thought the old woman might be asleep too, but she wasn't. She was over on the rough grass near the olive grove, with her goat. I trotted along the dirt track and joined her under the trees, and her wrinkled old face lit up when she saw me, as though I was a very dear friend. She started talking rapidly, and, although I could not understand, I knew she was saying nice things. I looked up at her.

"Mi padre," I said, "muy malo."

I had heard those words (and knew they meant "my father – very ill") many times – on the beach, at the inn and in the hospital, and now they had tremendous effect. The old lady was very upset and invited me in for "pan" and "leche", which I knew meant bread and milk. I had felt too restless for my dinner, so now I was hungry. I smiled and nodded and slipped my hand into hers, and we wandered back to the hut, with the goat skipping behind, occasionally butting me in the back in quite a friendly way.

The hut was bare and clean as before, and there was no sign of the grandchild. I was glad about this, for I wanted to be alone with the old woman. But I said nothing at first, for she was busy heating goats' milk on a little stove and cutting slices of bread. I looked round the simply furnished room while I enjoyed my meal. On an upturned box covered with a clean cloth lay the Bible. She sat watching me as I ate, smiling at me, and I wondered why she seemed to love me so, because I was quite an ordinary-looking child. But whatever the reason, I felt very welcome in her home, and as soon as I'd finished eating and drinking I went over to the Bible and put my hand on it and repeated, slowly and clearly, the words she had said to me: "Jesus es mi amigo."

She smiled even more, and then she pointed upwards, laid her hand over her heart and said "Jesus en mi corazón."

I stared, for once again I had understood. *Corazón* meant "heart", and I'd heard it at least twenty times in the last few hours. My father had had a heart attack; I'd heard about them before, because I once asked him why he swallowed so many pills, and why he walked so slowly, and why he didn't come swimming and he'd told me that he had a weak heart, and had to be careful. But when he'd seen little Concha sailing off toward the ocean he had not been careful... and that was why he was in hospital, and that was why Grandpa was coming.

*Jesus en mi corazón.* This seemed to describe what I'd been feeling. I suddenly remembered my Bible at home, and the picture in the front of it –

Jesus knocking at a door with weeds growing all over it. One day I'd asked Gran what door it was, and who he was trying to visit and she'd told me that it was a famous picture of Jesus knocking at the door of the human heart.* I hadn't been very interested, but now I suddenly felt that a light had shone on that picture.

"Come in," I whispered. "Oh please, please come in!" and then I realised that he'd been there ever since I'd asked him to be my friend, teaching me to care more about other people, making me want to know more about God and making me happier. He hadn't waited for me to put it into words, he'd just come to me as soon as I'd wanted him and cried out to him. I suddenly felt strong and glad and alive. I sat listening quietly while the old woman murmured on in Spanish, and though I couldn't understand a word it all sounded very peaceful and reassuring. After a while I kissed her and went home, for perhaps the telegram would have arrived, and it would soon be time to visit Daddy.

The telegram had arrived. All the children were running in all directions looking for me. Pepito saw me first and ran to meet me, his black eyes sparkling. He seized my hand and dragged me to the kitchen, where Lola produced the envelope and they all gathered round while I opened it.

"STARTING IMMEDIATELY STOP ARRIVING MALAGA 10.15 THURSDAY STOP GRANDPA."

* "The Light of the World" by W. Holman Hunt.

I read it over and over. Tomorrow by midday Grandpa would be here. With much talk and waving of hands Lola made me understand that she had an *amigo* in Malaga who would meet him and put him on the bus, and we would all go and wait for him in the market square.

I just could not wait to show my father the telegram. Lola had already been to the hospital to enquire, and they had said that he was better, so I set out alone, clutching the precious paper and counting the hours. It was nearly 5.00 pm; Grandpa would be here by dinner-time – about nineteen hours – and I'd be asleep for about nine of them. I climbed the cobbled streets to the hospital and found the kind old nun who said, "Come now. Your father – he better."

He really did look a little better although he still got tired quickly if he talked too much, so I talked to him instead, and showed him the telegram. I told him how lonely I was without him, and that I'd been to see the old woman and feasted on goats' milk and hot brown bread. He smiled.

"You do know how to look after yourself, don't you Lucita?" he said. "What did you and the old lady talk about this time?"

I looked down shyly.

"Tell me, Lucy. I like hearing about the old lady."

I looked up at him.

"She said, *'Jesus en mi corazón.'* I knew what that meant, because they all talk about your *corazón*. It means 'heart', doesn't it?"

"Well, yes. But perhaps not quite the same kind of heart..."

I wanted to ask him what he meant but he seemed rather breathless, so I talked about Grandpa's arrival next day. He seemed really glad to be seeing him, and when the nun came to take me away I skipped home without a care in the world because everything was going to be all right. I ran on the beach before going in for supper at the inn, and sat on a rock watching the colours on the sea while the sun went down behind the hills, and I prayed that my father's heart would get better quickly, and that he and my grandfather would become friends so we could all live happily ever after like one family.

It took me a long time to get to sleep that night. There was so much to think about – Daddy at the hospital, Grandpa probably already in London and Jesus in my heart. I knew he had lifted me to the safe shelter of his love, just as Lola would lift Concha to the safety and comfort of her arms whenever she was frightened or upset.

## Chapter Fifteen

## Grandpa arrives in Spain

Grandpa had never been out of England before, and I felt that anything might happen to him on his own in Spain, so we all went down to the market square much too early to meet him off the bus. At long last it swept round the corner and stopped in front of us, and there was Grandpa in his black Sunday suit and a big hat, peering short-sightedly into the crowd in every direction except the right one. He looked very English and out of place in Spain. I was in his arms before he'd even seen me, and Lola and the children were pressing round us, smiling and shaking hands, escorting him down the street that led to the inn, all talking Spanish all at once; and Grandpa followed, smiling and nodding and not understanding a word!

Only when he was comfortably seated in the

patio under the vine did we really greet each other. He had taken off his hat and coat and had a wash, and Lola had brought him a mug of chilled beer. He was feeling better and took a good look round.

"It's very warm here, isn't it Lucy?" he remarked. "And I must say you are looking well, though perhaps a little thinner. And how brown you are! And how's your poor father?"

I sat down beside him and talked and talked about Daddy – his kindness, his goodness, and his courage and how he had nearly given his life for Concha. And Grandpa sat watching me, his blue eyes rather troubled and anxious, but he did not interrupt me until I paused for breath.

"Your Gran, Lucy; she's quite well, but she finds it hard to settle when you're not there. She's just counting the days until you come home."

"Well, I won't be long," I replied. "Dad's getting better, and it's not long now until school. Tell me about home, Grandpa. How's the garden, and how's Shadow?"

He chatted on while I sat on the rug at his feet. I had not realised how much I'd missed home because there had been so much to think about, but now it was all coming back. I thought of all the sights and sounds around Pheasant Cottage, and Spain suddenly seemed very parched and hot.

Pepito and Pedro kept peeping through a crack in the door and being chased away by Lola and coming back again, but I hardly noticed them. Grandpa did, though, and called them in. He opened his case and presented them with a big bag of mixed sweets. They thanked him joyfully, and we could hear them for a long time talking excitedly in the kitchen. Then Lola came in with the dinner and insisted that Grandpa and I should eat alone together that first day. He pecked rather doubtfully at the spicy, oily food, but I ate an enormous meal and thoroughly enjoyed myself.

After lunch Grandpa had a long sleep for he said he had not slept a wink in his noisy London hotel, and he was feeling the heat, but at 5.00 pm we set out and walked up to the hospital almost in silence. Grandpa was obviously nervous, and kept clearing his throat and mopping his brow, and I was quiet because I was approaching the great moment of my life; Daddy and Grandpa were going to meet.

I hoped the old nun wouldn't take us up to the ward for I wanted to take Grandpa myself, and to my relief she wasn't there. The doorkeeper let us in, and nodded to the stairs. Grandpa was walking very slowly now, almost as though he were afraid, but I just could not wait. I ran ahead, slipped into the room without knocking and ran to my father.

"He's coming, Daddy," I announced. "Grandpa's coming up the stairs now. Are you ready?"

Grandpa's head came cautiously round the door and I wondered, for a moment, just what sort of a monster he expected to see! But at the sight of my father, so pale and weak, propped against pillows, his expression changed suddenly to one of great concern and compassion. He hurried across the room, both hands outstretched.

"Mr Martin," he cried, "how very, very sorry I am to see you like this... Lucy has been telling me about your... er... great courage in saving that

114

child." He had clasped Daddy's free hand, and Daddy was smiling his gentle, pleased smile, not the twisty one which meant he was making fun of someone. It was all going really well.

"Pull up that chair, Mr Ferguson," said my father. "I can't talk too much... get a bit breathless... but it's good to see you... Lucy, wait downstairs... I want to talk to Grandpa. Come and say goodbye later."

I trotted away and wandered round the old walled garden which smelled of thyme and lemon verbena. I felt very happy for everything was coming right. Daddy and I would soon go home together, and he would get better at Pheasant Cottage where it was cool and green. He could sit and write his books in the garden, and I would take him cups of coffee, and next summer we'd come back to Spain to Lola and Rosita and the children and the sea and the fishing boats and the old woman...

"Lucy, your father's waiting to say goodbye."

Grandpa was standing on the steps, and I ran to him joyfully. "Did you like him, Grandpa?" I asked. "I told you he was a good man, didn't I?"

"Yes, yes, Lucy; he's a good, brave man. Go to him now, but don't stay long. He's very tired."

I obeyed, but wondered why Grandpa seemed so distressed. And why were there tears in his eyes? Perhaps my father would tell me. I slipped into his room and hesitated; he lay so still, and his face was such a strange colour.

"Lucy, darling, come here." He managed to lift his arm and put it round me. "I wish I could explain, but I've been talking too long... I'll just have to tell you... I want you to go home with Grandpa tomorrow... you can't stay here alone... but I shall miss you. Hasn't it been a lovely holiday?"

My face flushed red. Leave him alone? It was impossible! I'd stay with Lola and visit him every day, and pack for him when he came home. But he pressed my hand.

"Lucy, darling, I'm too tired to argue," he said. "It's just got to be... Come in the morning and say goodbye... I'll explain then. And Lucy... never, never hate! What a stupid waste of time it all was... what a good old man he is!"

There was nothing more to be said. He kissed me and closed his eyes. I leaned against him for a moment or two, gulping back my tears, and then slipped away. As I came downstairs I could see Grandpa sitting on the bench in the hall waiting for me, but he did not hear my footsteps for he was thinking hard, with his head bowed. He looked such a sad old man. I suddenly felt afraid. What had gone wrong? They'd met and liked each other, and Daddy would get better and come home. I put my hand softly on Grandpa's shoulder, and he jumped.

"Grandpa," I whispered tearfully, "couldn't I wait until he's better? He'll need someone to carry his suitcase when he comes home. He's not allowed to carry anything heavy."

"You must do what he says, Lucy," said Grandpa, and his voice was sorrowful. "He told me in his telegram to book return seats. It's all for the best, my dear, but he'll find it hard to say goodbye in the morning, so you must help him by being brave and obedient."

We walked home almost in silence, and I left him
resting and went into the kitchen to tell Lola and
Rosita that I'd got to go home. Lola clasped me in
her arms and burst into tears, Rosita wrung her
hands and the little boys both cried together. We
wiped our eyes and fried potatoes and had a party.
Uncle played the guitar, Rosita danced and we all
sang. Grandpa was too tired to come so we took
him his supper on a tray. He was still feeling miserable.

"Grandpa," I whispered, "what's the matter?
Why are you so sad? He'll come soon, won't he?
And he can come to the cottage, can't he? You did
like him, didn't you, Grandpa?"

"Oh, yes, yes; oh dear, yes," said Grandpa, very
upset. "But what a lot of time we waste, Lucy,
when we won't forgive! I've been sitting here
thinking. I wasn't much good at book learning,
and your Gran could say it a lot better than I
could, but it seems to me that every hour when we
won't love and forgive, is an hour of life wasted.
And to think of all those years when we could have
done so much for him!"

"But you can do it now, Grandpa," I insisted.
"We'll all do lots for him when he comes home.
And do you think, Grandpa, that when he comes
we could go to the plane and meet him, you and
me? He shouldn't carry his suitcase himself, you
know!"

But Grandpa only said, "Please God we'll do all
we can for him, my dear," and went sadly to bed.
I did the same, but not to sleep. For this was the
last night I would watch the moonlight on my

white wall, or hear the break of small waves on the beach, or the muffled noises of the street in front of the inn; the footsteps and the chattering, the strumming of guitars from the cafés – all the sounds of Spain I had come to know so well. I had spent my last happy evening with Rosita and her family, and tomorrow I would pay my last visit to the hospital. I buried my face in the pillow and felt miserable, but soon fell asleep, and then I woke to my last sunny morning in Spain.

I had lots to do before we left in the afternoon. I had to pack all my Spanish treasures and visit my father and say goodbye to the old woman and have a farewell dinner with the family. I went with Rosita to fetch bread for the last time, but we kept wiping our eyes and sniffing, so it wasn't a very cheerful trip.

We had special permission to visit my father in the morning – me first, and Grandpa later. But I did not hurry on my way there; I walked slowly for I was dreading leaving him. But I knew it was too late to change anything, and the best way to help him was to obey as cheerfully as possible.

He had just had his morning wash and shave, and he looked fresher and brighter than he had the evening before. The room faced east and was full of sunshine, and a pleasant-looking young nun was bringing him a drink. I felt a bit more cheerful as I drew up a chair and leaned against the pillows.

"Daddy," I began, "I do wish I didn't have to leave you. Who'll visit you and look after you when I go?"

"Lola will visit me," he replied, "and I couldn't be better looked after anywhere. These nuns are wonderful, and that old one who comes in the afternoon tells me she goes to chapel and prays for me every day. I'm sure you'd approve of that!"

I turned to see if he was laughing, but his expression was quite serious and rather sad.

"That's two of us then Daddy," I said, "because I do too."

"Then keep right on, Lucita," he said gently, and we were silent for a few moments. He seemed tired with talking, so I talked instead. I told him all my wonderful plans for when he came home, and I described the summerhouse where he could sit and write with the clematis and honeysuckle climbing in at the window, and the robin who flew in and out of the spare bedroom which would be his. Grandpa had said so.

"So you see, they are longing for you to come," I finished. "You won't be long, will you?"

"I should love to come," he said, "only I can't be quite sure when. But remember, whatever happens in the future, nothing can ever take away this holiday. It's been the happiest time for me since your mother died. You've been such a perfect little companion, Lucy... it was like having her all over again... she didn't seem much older than you when I married her... you're so alike!"

"It's been a lovely holiday," I whispered, because my lips were trembling. "But... but ... it's been rather a sad ending, hasn't it?"

He held me as close as he could.

"Not really," he said, "in fact, I sometimes think it's the happiest ending possible. You see, I've often felt sad about those years when we could have been together... and all my own stupid fault...

so I'm glad I could give another little girl back to her parents... I often wake in the night and feel so thankful I got there just in time... and if I hadn't been ill I'd never have known your grandfather... It all came right, Lucy; such a happy ending!"

He was breathless with too much talking, and the young nun, who had been waiting outside, came over and put one hand gently on my shoulder and the other on my father's wrist. I gave him a last kiss, and she led me away, but at the door I turned and smiled through my tears.

"It was a lovely holiday," I said in a voice that only trembled slightly. "Thank you, Daddy, thank you so much!"

"And thank you too, Lucy; thank you so, so much!" he whispered, and then the door was closed softly behind me. I had said goodbye.

I did not want to go straight back to the house. Why, oh why did I have to leave him just when he needed me so much to visit him and to fetch things and to pack his suitcase when he got better? Almost without knowing it, my feet had been carrying me across the marketplace towards the vineyards and the olive trees. Each time I'd gone there I'd found comfort, and now I needed it more than ever before.

The grape harvest had begun, and my old woman was there amongst the vines working hard, her little granddaughter beside her. There were other people there too, and they stared curiously at me as I slipped towards her through the bushes. When she saw me she threw up her hands in delight, and pressed a grape into my mouth. Then she looked at me more closely and knew that I was in trouble. She squatted on the warm soil by her loaded basket and drew me down beside her. The vines made a private shelter round us, and I tried to tell her my sad story. My father, I explained, was still in hospital. Pointing upwards to the sky, I said I was going to England in an *avión*. I'd come to say *adiós*. My eyes filled with tears again.

She understood at once, and murmured her sympathy. Some of the words she spoke back to me I could understand.

"Jesus... with me." "Jesus... with you." "Jesus... with your father."

Of course – I understood! In my sadness I'd forgotten. I wasn't leaving Daddy alone. I was leaving him with Jesus, who loved him very much, and who, so far, had made everything come right and answered my prayers. He'd been there in the quiet ward, and even if my father didn't know much about him, he knew all about my father. And the old nun was praying for him, and I was, too, and my grandfather liked him. All was well.

I picked two vine leaves to press in memory of that moment, kissed the old woman and left her sadly. She looked as if she was calling down heaven's blessings on my head. Then I remembered something that made me clap my hands softly, and skip down the dirt track. I was going home to Gran and Shadow!

## Chapter Sixteen

## "All bright in front..."

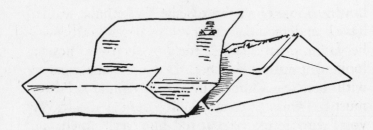

As soon as we got home Grandpa told our vicar about my father, and he immediately got in touch with an English chaplain in the south of Spain who held services for visitors all through the summer, and he started to visit my father and send us news.

It was on a day that we received a letter from him that Gran gave us a real surprise.

We were sitting at the window table eating our lunch on that ordinary September day, when Gran suddenly put down her knife and fork and said, "It's no use, Herbert! I just can't stand it any longer!"

"Stand what, Elsie?" said Grandpa, getting up in alarm. "Is there something wrong with the meat pie?"

"Certainly not," said Gran, "I made it myself. It's just that I can no longer stand the thought of that poor, brave husband of Alice's being in a foreign country with no family around him. If we sold the antique cabinet I could go and put things right."

"Well, if you feel like that, you must go, Elsie. But you mustn't sell the antique cabinet – that's been in your family for hundreds of years. I could sell some of the hens. They are a valuable breed."

"Nonsense, Herbert," replied Gran, "you know how much you love those hens! The cabinet was to have been left to Lucy, but I'm sure she'd rather see her father properly cared for. No Lucy – it's no use looking at me like that because you are not coming with me! School starts in a week's time and you must help take care of your Grandpa. You know you'll never remember to take your medicine unless someone reminds you, Herbert. It's not that I want to leave you, but I don't like to think of that poor, dear man stranded in a place where no one speaks a word of English."

I stared at her in amazement. No one had called him a "poor, dear man" when he was in prison! But there was no doubt about it, something had happened. We had become a family.

Gran was a woman of action. She visited the vicar that very afternoon, who phoned the English chaplain, who promised to meet her and find somewhere for her to stay. Four days later, Gran set off in her best clothes, with her overcoat over her arm, as she would not believe how hot it was. Grandpa took her to the airport, and I stayed the night with Mary.

I was very glad to see Grandpa back, and we settled down to look after each other, although he almost lived from one letter to the next. Gran wrote nearly every day and seemed to be enjoying herself. She was actually staying with the English chaplain and went to the hospital twice a day where she read aloud to my father and took down messages from him for me.

"But why can't he read himself, Grandpa?" I asked. "And why can't he write to me himself yet?"

"I don't imagine he's strong enough," said Grandpa, looking distressed. And I think it was after that that we stopped talking about Daddy coming home.

I missed Gran a lot, but it was very relaxed living with Grandpa. I was enjoying reading my Bible now, and going to church on Sunday. It seemed different, not just an old building where I had to go with my grandparents, but my friend Jesus' house, where I could talk to him. The words of the service meant so much more – "I believe in the Lord, the Giver of Life."

Life! I'd been so near death that the very word was precious. Concha had nearly lost her life. My father had looked so still and grey on the beach, but he'd lived; then there was the figure on the crucifix at the hospital – Jesus – and he had come back from death.

After dinner one night I went to my favourite seat on the rockery behind a screen of hollyhocks, and started to read the Gospel of John. I read very slowly on into the third chapter, "For God loved the world so much that he gave his only Son, so that everyone who believes in him may not die but have eternal life."*

* John 3:16. Good News Bible.

I looked round. Everything was dying but it didn't seem important because everywhere there were signs of new life. The butterflies on the Michaelmas daisies had once been caterpillars, but each one had rolled into a chrysalis, then at last had come bursting out as a bright butterfly.

"In him was life," and as I read, I understood, although I could not possibly have put it into words. My friend Jesus had not only lived on earth, and healed the sick, and been kind to children. He was also God, and he had given me everlasting life. I thought of Daddy, and wished that he could believe, too.

A week after Gran left I went back to school and enjoyed telling my friends about all my adventures in Spain. I also showed off by speaking a little Spanish to them!

I was very busy helping Grandpa in the house and doing my homework, but I tried to read a little of John's Gospel every day. I had got up to chapter 11. One Saturday, a fortnight after the beginning of term, I went to the woods with Shadow, taking my Bible with me. It was the first of October, and I was excited for I knew Don would be home for the weekend. I hadn't seen him since my holiday.

I picked some blackberries then sat on a tree trunk and read John chapter 11. Jesus said, "I am the resurrection and the life. Whoever believes in me will live, even though he dies; and whoever lives and believes in me will never die. Do you believe this?"* The flowers' petals fell off, and

---

* John 11:26. Good News Bible.

seeds fell to the ground and were buried by leaves, but the Spring always came again, with fresh growth. I put my Bible back in my pocket and went home, thinking about the apple and black-berry pie I would make for supper.

"Grandpa," I called at the front door, "where are you? I'll get dinner."

There was no answer. I glanced into the living room and there he was sitting at the table, his face buried in his hands, an open letter in front of him. I stopped dead.

"Grandpa," I cried, "what's the matter?" and Shadow, sensing trouble, trotted forward, and laid his nose on Grandpa's knee.

He looked up quickly and his eyes were full with tears.

Then I knew, and realised I'd known deep down ever since Gran had gone away. This was what I'd really been waiting for, and this was why life and death had seemed so important.

"My dear, dear, Lucy," said Grandpa, "I don't know how to tell you..."

"It's Daddy, isn't it?" I whispered, for my throat felt rather dry. "He's dead, isn't he?" Then I ran into Grandpa's arms and we cried together and Shadow licked us frantically in turn.

"He died on Wednesday," said Grandpa at last, "but Gran didn't phone because he wanted you to have this letter as soon as you knew. He knew he couldn't last long. That was why he wanted you to leave – he wanted you safe and settled at home when you got the news. He wrote this letter just a little at a time on the days when he felt better. Would you like to read it here with me, Lucy, or would you like to take it away by yourself?"

"I think I'd like to read it alone," I said, drying my eyes on Grandpa's handkerchief. "Do you mind if I go back into the wood for a bit?"

"Not at all, dearie; just come and have your lunch when you're ready," said Grandpa, so I clutched my letter and went out, with Shadow trotting quietly beside me, trying to comfort me.

It seemed so strange reading a letter from someone who had died. I went back to my tree trunk and looked round me. Autumn had come early that year and the trees were glorious in their dying colours. The silver birches were pale gold and the horse chestnut a vivid yellow. Acorns and shining conkers lay among the leaves, seeds of life waiting to send up their shoots of new life. I drew a deep breath and opened my letter.

It was quite long. He had written on different days, in rather shaky handwriting. He told me how much he loved me, and how sorry he was about the years we'd missed when we might have been together. He spoke of Gran, and how good she'd been, how thankful he was that we'd all got to know each other, how glad he was to leave me in such good care. I read very slowly, for the letter was nearly finished now, and he hadn't told me what I so wanted to know.

I drew another deep breath and read the last paragraph.

"Don't be sad, Lucita. It's the best, happiest ending. I want to tell you that I now know that we shall see each other again – you, me, your mother. Jesus came just in time. The chaplain was a help, but it was you who first showed me, on the beach that day. It's like you said, the cross is behind and it's all bright in front…"

The writing trailed off as though he had been too tired to finish the letter. He had probably meant to go on, but he had written all I wanted to know. A robin on a mountain ash tree suddenly sang for joy, and I looked up, through my tears, at the blurred gold and crimson sunlight. Daddy was right – it was all bright in front. He had passed through death into life beyond – from winter to springtime, and for me, too, nothing would ever be the same again. Daddy had opened up to me a whole new world. I'd seen the sea; I'd learned to love Spain and poetry, and Lola and Rosita. One day I would go back, and best of all I'd found out the real secret of eternal life. In Jesus there was life, now and for ever.

Shadow suddenly barked. I brushed away my tears and looked up again. Don was racing through the wood on his way to the cottage, a living bounding creature leaping over the crimson brambles. He turned his head and saw me.

"Hurrah, Lucy!" he shouted. "All safe home at last!" – and although he didn't know it then, his greeting had a special deeper meaning.

My mum and dad were both safe home at last – together.

For ever.